State of Chaos

Collapse Series #2

Summer Lane

Summer Lane

WB Publishing

2nd Edition

Praise for *State of Emergency* (Collapse Series #1)

"I sat down to read State of Emergency and found myself unable to stop. The characters were well developed, the story constantly kept me on edge and I found myself quickly compelled to read more. Most novels take me about a week to read. I finished State of Emergency within two nights."

- Ruth Silver, Write Away Bliss and Author of Aberrant

"It was very compelling, and I enjoyed it all the way! You [Summer Lane] are quite a talented writer with an amazing gift for narration. Congratulations on a book well done!"

- Janice White, Author and Editor

"This book is awesomesauce. Literally. Summer effortlessly tells the story of one girl's need to survive whatever has happened to her country. She paints a realistic picture of the what if."

– Hannah Membrey, *The Girl in a Café*

"Even though SOE is a full length novel, I read it so fast—because I needed more!—that, when I finished, I felt like I had read a novella. It was fast paced, surprising, romancy, thrilling. A great book from the first word to the last!"

– Juliana Haygert, author of Destiny Gift, Her Heart's Secret Wish and His Allure, Her Passion

"State of Emergency is written with an assured and strong voice and the narrative moves (like the car Chris and Cassie escape, and LA thrown into chaos) with considerable speed; building tension and momentum with every turn of the kindle page."

– Summer Day, author of Pride & Princesses & Wuthering Nights

"I felt these two were quite likeable interesting characters, and I was impressed by Summer's writing style. I can't wait for the sequel to SOE. I rate this fantastic book five stars."

- Mark Mackey, author of Curse Girl

"State of Emergency does its job very well! It thrills you, it scares you, it keeps you reading like crazy because you just have to see what happens next, and, most important of all, it makes you feel. And that is not an easy feat for a book. I'm REALLY looking forward to reading what happens in the next book!"

- Karla V., Not Just Nonsense

"I loved pretty much everything about this book. The pacing was great, and I never once got bored. There was always something happening to keep things interesting, whether it was meeting strange people, trying to survive, or action scenes. I loved it."

– Briana Snyder, Reviewer

"Summer Lane knows how to keep you on the edge of your seat! This book is just one cliff hanger after another...Cassidy is a strong willed and strong minded girl with sharp wit and a mouth full of sassy comebacks. I absolutely loved her. The secondary MC, Chris - the incredibly hot navy seal who saves the sassy Cassidy's butt on several occasions is swoon worthy and written very well."

– Bonnie Rae, author of The Nether Trilogy

"State of Emergency is an engaging read that is compelling and believable. Some dystopian novels are so far removed from reality that it makes it difficult for the reader to connect with the story; not the case with State of Emergency. It's fast paced and enjoyable. If you like this genre, then you will love this book."

- Roy Huff, author of the bestselling *Everville Saga Series*

For Rocklin, my best friend.

Prologue

I remember when I had a life. Sure, it wasn't perfect by any stretch, but at least it was *something*. I had a nice house, a car, and a stack of books in my closet that rivaled the leaning tower of Pisa. I didn't have any friends, but I had a father. I didn't have any money, but I was working on that.

It was normal.

I don't know what "normal" is anymore. Before an electromagnetic pulse disabled the country, I thought the worst crisis that could possibly hit my world was my parent's divorce or accidentally draining the battery in the car overnight.

I was so wrong.

Life is nothing like it used to be. Things used to be easy. Flip a switch? On goes the light. Press a button? You're calling your parents. Swipe a credit card? You just paid for lunch. Easy, simple, convenient. Nothing is like that anymore. People are dying, starving. They're being *executed* on the streets. A shadow army called Omega is rolling its forces across the country, imprisoning and killing everybody or anything that gets in its way. I don't know where *our* military is, but there are rumors that they're fighting Omega on the East Coast.

So what does that mean for the folks in California? Folks like me? It means we're on our own. I would be dead right now if it weren't for the help of Chris Young, the most amazing guy I've ever met and a Navy SEAL to boot. But we've lost our families. They're imprisoned somewhere in the city, arrested as war criminals for committing one simple crime: They survived the takeover.

Chris's family – his parents and brother, Jeff – were kind to me. My own dad was taken along with them, and what happened to my estranged mother is anybody's guess. We lost a friend of ours to Omega, too. Isabel, a twelve year-old girl we rescued from an abandoned McDonald's.

Things suck right now.

It's just me and Chris, toughing it out in the foothills of the Sierra Nevada Mountains, trying to stay off the Omega radar. Because according to them, we're wanted fugitives. Our experience with them hasn't been positive, and we've nearly been killed more times than I care to count.

So what happens now? Do we give up? Do we live the rest of our lives sleeping in the dirt, starving? Do we let Omega take our families and rip everything that's important to us out of our lives?

No. Chris wants to fight Omega – literally and figuratively speaking. I just want to find our families and get the heck out of Omega's crosshairs. But to do that, we have to *find* our folks first. And so far there's only one place we can think of that Omega would bring war criminals:

The city.

We have to go back.

Chapter One

Have you ever hiked in the mountains? Here's how it works: You climb uphill on little known dirt trails, fight your way through poison ivy and avoid hornet nests hiding in dead logs. By the time you reach your destination, you're sweating, thirsty and hungry. So you eat a picnic lunch, take photos of your memorable experience in the great outdoors, and head back home. Just like that, the physical strain has ended, and you're comfortable again.

For me? Not so much.

My life has been a perpetual walk-a-thon since December of last year. And considering it's now February, I'm reasonably tired of it. A picnic lunch is sounding *really* good right about now.

But I never get a break. Even now, I'm pushing my way through a field of golden grass in the foothills, below what used to be Sequoia National Park. It's freezing – there's ice on the ground – and the sun is coming up over the horizon.

"Could you slow down and let me catch my breath?" I pant, placing my hands against my waist. "Hey! Rambo!"

Chris turns around. He shoves stray pieces of hair away from his face, unmoved by my request. He's wearing a wool shirt under a thick leather jacket, pants tucked into his combat boots. His hair is pulled tight into a ponytail, accentuating the angles of his face.

"Sweat it out, Cassie," he says. "We're almost there."

"How far is almost?"

"Close enough."

"'Close enough' in *civilian* speak or *SEAL* speak?"

He snorts, unconsciously flexing the muscles in his arms, and starts walking again. At six foot four, he towers over me by more than a foot, which makes it even harder for me to keep up with his pace. One of his steps is nearly equal to three of mine.

"You could at least make your strides smaller," I say, jogging beside him. "I can't keep up."

He rolls his eyes. Even in the near darkness he looks handsome, his beard thicker than it used to be, his green eyes bright against his dirty blonde hair. He's also ten years older me, and I like to think of him as my boyfriend.

Technically, labeling someone your "boyfriend" at this point in time is about as worthless as paper money, but I like to pretend that at least one thing in our situation is normal. Chris is twenty-eight. I'm nineteen. He's a former Navy SEAL with a serious reputation for kicking butt.

I, on the other hand, am an abandoned young adult with a reputation for complaining about cold temperatures and suffering obscene taco cravings. And trust me, since there's no such thing as Taco Bell anymore, I've been left with serious withdrawals.

"It's insane anyway," I mutter. "We'll never make it there in one piece."

"We don't have a choice." He shoots me a stern, disciplinary look. I get that a lot from him. "You know that."

I exhale, creating a small white cloud over my mouth.

"Yeah. I know."

And I do. I just didn't think we'd be able to come to a decision to pull it off.

Rescue our families from Omega, I mean.

When the electromagnetic pulse hit in December, the world pretty much died. The *modern* world, that is. An electromagnetic pulse, or an EMP, is an invisible energy wave that disables all forms of technology based in computer mechanics. Your cellphone, your laptop, your television, your cars, your generators, your radios. Everything dies instantly. Nothing works. Helicopters, airplanes, buses, trains, trucks, satellites, you name it. Anything with a computer chip. And the worst part of it is that once something's been hit with an EMP, it's fried forever. You can't revive a computer once it's been killed. It's gone. An EMP can be caused by a nuclear explosion in the atmosphere – or even something as simple as a solar flare.

Where did *this* EMP come from?

I don't know. That's the big question.

An EMP hit the entire United States. For all I know, it could have hit the whole world. I was in Culver City, California when it happened. Right down the street from Hollywood and Wilshire Boulevard ordering Chinese takeout. Planes fell out of the sky like bombs. Everyone panicked. I only got out of the city because my dad, as a military guy and a doomsday prepper (yeah, I had one of *those* parents), always insisted that we be prepared in the case of a national emergency.

I threw my emergency go-bags in the back of an old Mustang – an EMP-proof vehicle because it doesn't have a computer based electronic ignition – and booked it. I was separated from my dad in the chaos that ensued, but we'd had a plan in place in case anything like this ever happened:

Meet at our family cabin in the mountains.

Plans rarely pan out. Especially for me. I'm a bad karma magnet, something Chris can attest to. I met him when I was escaping the city. He was wounded, I helped him, and in exchange for a ride to his family's home in the foothills, he helped me survive.

Unfortunately, my car was stolen by a group of desperate rioters. We were forced to travel on foot, and in the process, we passed near Omega emergency relief camps. We saw them for what they really were: concentration camps. Places where Omega could remove unwanted remnants of society. Civilians that they deemed violent, inciting or useless.

Chris and I came to the conclusion that Omega sent out the EMP as an excuse to take control of everything and yeah…they pulled it off.

Long story short, Chris and I are on the run from Omega. My dad, as far as I know, was taken by Omega officials and imprisoned as a war criminal because he wouldn't go to a "relief camp." Chris's family, his parents and his brother, were taken, too. Their house was burned down. A friend of ours named Isabel was also arrested.

So now it's just the two of us.

We've been keeping a low profile in the foothills for two months. Omega officials would love to arrest us, to send us to one of their many concentration camps. But we're not really into the whole execution-without-a-trial thing.

We want to live, thank you very much.

We're not even criminals. The only thing that sets us apart from the masses is that we chose to avoid the concentration camps and stayed off the radar rather than take the bait. That makes us a target, I guess. Anomalies.

Sucks to be us.

Chris, as a Navy SEAL and a special ops guy, has kept us fed. He can make a meal out of a piece of grass. It might not be great for the taste buds, but his skills have kept us alive. I'm learning from him, too.

I'm good at finding shelter, locating at least *something* edible, and judging potentially hazardous situations. In the end, it is ultimately Chris's knowledge and skills that have gotten us this far. Alone, I would have died long ago. Together, we thrive. We help each other. We provide moral support for the other. We're a team.

Before the EMP, his superiority would have bothered me. I would have felt useless and insecure. But since my life depends on things like finding food or avoiding getting shot by an Omega soldier, I just don't go there. Petty issues have no place in my life anymore.

Conversely, Chris is *way* out of my league. If we hadn't been forced together when the end of the world came crashing down around our ears, there's not a chance he would have been romantically interested in me. A guy like him and a girl like me? It wouldn't have happened. Chris, if doomsday hadn't popped in to pay us a visit, would be most likely be dating a hot swimsuit poster girl for the Navy otherwise.

He's *that* gorgeous.

To me, at least.

When you're in love with someone, it's hard to see their flaws. And although I know Chris cares about me, I can't get rid of the feeling that he's only interested in me because we've been forced together. Literally. Our families are both imprisoned somewhere, if not dead, and we're the only ones who care enough to find them. We need each other, and that makes the lines between friendship and romance blur. I mean, *you* spend twenty-four seven with somebody for three months and see what happens.

So what's our plan? How are we even going to find the prison or camp that our families have been taken to?

We don't really know.

We just figure that Omega will bring them somewhere they can publicize it, where they can make an example of their "war criminals" and scare people into submission.

There's only one place we can go to look for our families: the city. But *what* city? What *state*? What *building*? It's an impossible rescue mission, but thinking about it and working towards it – even if it's never going to happen – gives us something to hold onto.

It gives us hope.

Chapter Two

My grandfather used to quote,

"Give me a ship and a star to sail her by."

Well, *I* just want a car. Any car. A decrepit piece of junk from someone's backyard would be better than what we have: Nothing.

Nothing but our feet. Nothing but socks worn through with holes. Nothing but endless walking and moving and hunting and scraping to survive. I'm tired of eating scraps in the wilderness. I want a hamburger. I want ice cream. I want something with *calories.*

Unfortunately for me, the rations in my backpack aren't doing anything to grant my wish. After two months in the foothills, all I've got left is a handful of camping materials, water purifying tablets, a knife (a gift from Chris's brother, Jeff) and a plastic bag with one serving of coffee.

Lately we've been doing our hiking, hunting or foraging – whatever we're doing to keep alive – during the night. It keeps us from freezing to death by staying active, and it's easier for us to avoid detection if we're not moving across an open field in broad daylight.

Right now it's barely dawn. Streams of early morning sunlight are breaking through the fog, giving everything a ghostly in-between appearance of day and night. On the edge of the field stands a worn chain link fence. It's the property line of a trailer park, and for us, it's going to be our camping area all day.

"I hope there aren't any creeps hanging around here," I murmur.

"They won't live long," Chris replies.

I wait for him to smile. He doesn't.

I decide to blame it on exhaustion as we approach the chain link fence surrounding the property. It's falling apart in some places so we're able to squeeze between gaps between the metal. The trailer park is dotted with trees and picnic benches. Useless cars are parked near most of the houses, and by the looks of the broken blinds in a few of the windows – and the condition of some of the trailers – it's hard to tell if everything's been vandalized since the EMP or if this was simply a bad area.

There are no voices, no sounds. But it's early and most people, if there's anyone here, will be sleeping at this hour. Chris waves me forward as we creep between the trailers, pausing beneath windows or doors, listening for sounds. How are we supposed to tell if there are occupants inside? I whisper this question into Chris's ear.

He shrugs. "Look through the window."

"Are you kidding? *All* of your tactical knowledge and expertise comes down to sticking my head through a window?"

"Look, I'm tired," he says, stifling a yawn. "I checked this place out earlier."

"What? When?"

"When you fell asleep last night...when you were *supposed* to be keeping watch."

"Ah. Right." I cough. "Sorry."

"Go ahead," he says, challenging me. "Look."

I sigh. He does this often; forces me to do things I'm not comfortable with. Must be a military thing. I creep underneath a trailer window, slowly bringing my eyes over the windowsill. I peer through the dirty glass, seeing nothing but an empty living room.

"Looks safe," I say, giving him a thumbs up.

Chris nods.

"It is." He stands up and strolls up to the front door, working with the doorknob for a few seconds before popping the lock. "After you."

"Are you trying to get me killed?"

He finally laughs.

"Cassie, I was here earlier. I wouldn't send you into a trailer cold turkey, would I? I'm just messing with you."

I raise an eyebrow. He chuckles again, swinging the door open and taking the first few steps into the trailer. I wait at the threshold, listening for suspicious sounds. I stifle a scream when Chris jumps out of the shadows, grabbing my shoulders. "Gotcha."

I rake my hands through my hair, heart racing.

"That was *not* funny," I say. "I really didn't need that."

"Yeah, you did. Don't let your guard down for a second. Remember that."

"I'll remember."

Chris slides two fingers under my chin, tilting my head up.

"I'm just trying to help you," he says, kissing my forehead. "Come on. Let's eat."

I lick my lips, wondering how a guy so *logical* can get so much enjoyment out of scaring the crap out of me.

Only a man.

"Dusty," I remark, wrinkling my nose and closing the door behind me. The trailer home looks nearly thirty years old, complete with wallpaper from the 80s. There's a tiny kitchen, a living room with puke green carpet and a hallway in the back of the house.

"I don't think this place has been cleaned since it was built," I say.

"Probably an accurate assumption," Chris replies, dropping his gear on a couch. "Whoever was living here is long gone."

"What about food and water?"

"Let's check it out." Chris shrugs his jacket off, keeping his favorite knife sheathed in a strap around his thigh. "Here." He helps me remove my backpack, rubbing my sore shoulders for a moment. I lean against his chest, finding myself wrapped into a warm hug.

"You don't hug me enough," I sigh.

I feel his mouth turn up into a smile against my forehead. He draws his hands up my arms, pausing to assess me. "You're right," he says at last, his green eyes sparkling with amusement. "I don't."

I tap his cheek.

"Come on. Let's get some dinner."

Chris feigns disappointment when I slip out of his embrace and walk into the kitchen. It smells stale and pungent. Dirty coffee mugs are sitting in a sink that dried up long ago. Sticky notes and magnets are stuck on a dead fridge.

"I wonder who lived here," I whisper. "I wonder how old they were."

Chris leans against the doorframe, watching me carefully. I bend down and open the oak cabinets, finding dishes and junk. There's nothing in the fridge that's not already rotten, but in a cupboard above the dishwasher, Chris finds canned goods.

"What have we here?" he muses, tossing me a can.

"Pears!" I exclaim, excited. "And beans. Okay, wait. Pears, beans *and* soup."

"But what kind of soup? That's the question."

"Corn chowder. It's still good."

"Let's get cooking then."

So we do. As strange as it is to camp inside someone's old trailer home, I adjust quickly. Anything's better than sleeping outdoors again. The winter has been brutal – lots of rain, snow and fog. Being able to take my shoes off and walk around on the carpet feels great. No mud, no ice, and no bugs.

It's a luxury I haven't had in a long time.

Chris is in an unusually good mood, which means he finds plenty of reasons to tease me about my non-existent cooking skills. But let's face it. There's not a lot you can do with canned food during an apocalypse.

"Smells good," Chris says, studying a heavy mirror in the living room. "Hey, Cassidy...?"

I turn.

"What?"

"Have you ever left a secret message in a mirror?"

"Please. That's a Boy Scout trick."

"Boy Scout?" Chris feigns an offended expression. "Honey, I wasn't just a Boy Scout. I was an Eagle Scout." He leans against the wall. "I used to leave messages for my brother in the mirror..." he trails off, swallowing.

Silence fills the room. I know what he's thinking.

Is his brother even alive?

I blink back tears and get back to cooking.

There's no electricity, obviously, but the gas line to the house is still good. All I have to do is open the burner and light the stove with a match. I'm cooking the beans and soup in one of the pots I found above the sink.

"Hand me those bowls, will you?" I ask, gesturing to a stack of plastic mixing bowls I dug out of the cupboards. "We'll split everything."

I give a bowl of soup and beans to Chris, and I take what's left of it.

"Gourmet food," I say, raising my bowl in a toast. "Cheers."

"Cheers." Chris can't find any silverware so we tip the bowls back and sip the hot food. It's delicious, and it trumps eating a field rodent any day.

"So what now?" I ask, the two of us lounging on the beat up sofa in the living room. "Do we move in here?"

"Not a bad idea, actually," Chris smiles. "I can think of worse things than being trapped in a confined space with you."

"Wow. Just wow," I say, smirking. But I'm acting. I love it when he flirts with me. "I'm serious. What's our next move?"

"There's not a lot we can do." Chris finishes the rest of his soup, rubbing his chin. "We don't know where they are. We don't even know if they're -"

"-Don't," I interrupt. "They're *alive.*"

Chris says nothing. He picks up our empty bowls and walks into the kitchen. I get a sinking feeling in my stomach every time we bring this up, but we can't wander aimlessly in the wilderness forever. We have to have a *plan*. We need to at least find someplace to live so we don't freeze to death when winter comes around again.

"What if they took them to Los Angeles?" I say.

"What if they took them to San Jose? Or San Bernardino? Or San Francisco?" Chris stalks out of the kitchen, clearly frustrated. "They could be anywhere. We don't have a choice but to stay here and be smart, Cassidy. Impulsive action will get us killed. We have to be patient and thoughtful. We can't rush into *anything*."

I fold my arms around my knees, pressing my face into my legs. Over the past couple of months, I've stopped crying about losing Dad and the Young family. I'm numb. The pain of being separated from them is an underlying current, a constant stress. Yet it's amazing how fast I've adjusted to living in a post-apocalyptic world. How quickly I've accepted the present situation for the norm.

"Cassie?" Chris gently slides his hands through my hair, pushing back the scarf tied around my forehead for warmth. "We can't go looking for people who've completely vanished. Our focus right now is *surviving*. If we put ourselves in unnecessary danger, we'll get killed."

"Is that what they taught you in the Navy?" I ask.

"Yes." He pauses. "I'm sizing up the odds, Cassie. They're not in our favor."

"But -"

"-They're not in our favor *yet*. Don't give up. We're alive, right?"

"Yeah. Big deal."

He frowns. "It is. A lot of people would love to be us."

I crawl forward and lay my head against his chest, listening to his steady heartbeat. It's kind of a summary of who Chris is as a person: Steady. Reliable. Confident.

Logical.

"What do we do until then?" I whisper. "What about what we talked about? We were going to rescue them. What are we supposed to do if we don't?"

"We *stay* alive," he replies, wrapping his arms around me, tracing his fingers down the curve of my back. "Deal?"

I nod.

"Deal."

I enjoy a temporary feeling of security with those words. Granted, I don't really believe that everything's going to be rainbows and lollipops if we start thinking positively, but we need to focus on one thing at a time.

I fall asleep snuggled into Chris's warmth, lulled to sleep by his breathing and the sound of a strong wind slapping tree branches against the trailer roof. At around four in the morning, Chris stirs, stretching one arm behind his head.

"Could be another storm," he murmurs, his voice heavy with sleep. "You warm enough?"

I shrug.

He leaves the couch, walking into the hallway. Out of respect – and maybe a little bit of superstition – I haven't ventured into the bedrooms of the house yet. It seems wrong, somehow.

"Where are you doing?" I ask.

"Getting blankets," he calls back, and I hear him moving stuff around. Curiosity gets the better of me and I walk across the living room, still sleepy. I poke my head into the first bedroom. There's a king size bed and a matching dresser. Pictures have been taken off the wall, but besides that, it looks like most of the belongings of the couple that lived here are still intact.

"What I'd give to sleep in a bed," I remark.

"So do it." Chris kicks his boots off, rolling onto the mattress. "I forgot what it was like to sleep on a bed. Get over here, Cassidy."

"I'm not sleeping on a *bed* with you."

"*In* a bed with me." He pulls back the covers, waving me over. "It's warm."

I roll my eyes, looking over the contents of the dresser. A string of faux pearls is hanging on a jewelry tower. A half-empty perfume bottle is tilted sideways against a wooden box of earplugs and defunct hearing aids.

Apparently the former residents of this home were elderly.

"I wonder where they went," I say. "If they took all their stuff, maybe they had a working car."

"Probably." Chris spreads his arms across the pillows. "Cassidy?"

"Hmm?"

"Come here."

My hand hovers over a stainless steel bracelet etched with the name *Annalisa*. I slip it over my wrist, realizing how long it's been since I've worn any jewelry. Well, besides the necklace Chris gave me...and I put it back. I can't bring myself to take anything out of this house. It's just not *right*.

I walk over to Chris. He's got a wry expression on his face.

"Trying to seduce me?" I say, raising an eyebrow.

"Obviously." Chris offers a handsome smile, hooking his thumbs around my belt loops, pulling me forward. "What are you so afraid of?"

I swallow, suddenly feeling *very* warm. I brace myself against his shoulders. Chris leans up and kisses the bottom of my chin. I close my eyes, relaxing into him, just as he presses his lips against mine. The heat of the kiss is intense – different than when I kissed him earlier – as he pulls me closer, tighter. I link my hands together behind his neck. He rubs comforting circles into my arms.

"Chris," I say, breaking the embrace.

Finding my breath again.

"Mmm?" He strokes the side of my face with his finger.

"I'm sleeping on the couch."

"Oh, yeah?" He grins, sitting up, holding me in his lap. "And miss out on all this?"

"Exactly," I say, hot. "I just...I'm tired. Okay?"

"Really?" Chris looks amused. "Come on. Stay."

"No."

He presses the tip of his nose against mine, closing his eyes.

"I've been sleeping beside you for months," he says. "Whether it's in the snow or on a bed doesn't really make a difference, does it?"

I take a shaky breath.

"This is different," I insist.

And it is. If there's one thing I know about Chris, he does things *all the way*. He doesn't stop. He's the logical, steady man when it comes to any situation except...well, *this*. I may – possibly – be in love with the man, but I'm only nineteen. He's twenty-eight, he's ready for this kind of thing. And I'm not.

Not yet.

"Sorry," I say, kissing his forehead. "But it's the couch for me."

"Cassie," he replies, laughter rumbling in his chest. "I'm not going to-"

"-Don't even say it!" I cut in. "Please."

"Say *what*?"

Thank God it's dark in here. I'm blushing fire engine red.

"I'm not talking about *that* with you," I say, shifting back.

"You're too easy to read, Cassie." He grins again. "*Extremely* easy."

"Not that easy." I swing my legs around and sit on the edge of the bed. "I'm just saying...I don't..." I rub my temples. "Never mind. Goodnight."

Unperturbed, Chris keeps his arms around my waist.

"Trust me," he says.

I face him. His voice is soft. He's making it hard to say no to him. "Fine," I reply, squeezing his hand. "I trust you."

I slip under the heavy quilt of the bed – a *real* blanket! – and Chris lays his arm across the pillow. I rest my head against his bicep, comfortable lying close enough to take in his scent of spice and coffee.

"Goodnight, Cassidy," he says, his voice teasing. Fingering my shirt.

"Goodnight."

As I fall asleep, all I can think is,

One of these days I'm going to get the hang of this love thing.

The next morning I wake up alone. Groggy, I sit up and make a note of the fact that it's gray and foggy outside. For the fifty-millionth time.

"Chris?" I slip out of the covers and place my feet on the floor, yawning. I glimpse my reflection in the dresser mirror. Bad hair day.

Bad hair *month.*

"What are you doing?" I ask, stepping into the living room. Chris is dressed in his jacket and boots, checking his weapons – or as I like to call them, his "arsenal of awesome."

"Chris?" I fold my arms over my chest, glancing at his face. "What's wrong? Are we in trouble?"

"Nothing's wrong, Cassie," he grins. "Relax."

"Then what's up with all the weaponry?"

"I'm hungry." He gestures towards the kitchen. "I need more than veggies and soup to keep alive. I'm going hunting. You stay here, okay?"

"You could be gone for hours."

"Most likely."

He slings his gun over his back, picking up a few more, leaving me with a couple of knives and a rifle that's nearly twice my size. "Go back to bed. Get some rest. You've earned it."

"Can't I come?"

Chris shakes his head, fighting a smile.

"No. Stay here and rest." He moves in to press a kiss against my cheek. "See you later. Do *not* leave the trailer. Don't draw attention to yourself. I'll be back by sundown."

"And if you're not?"

"You stay here and wait for me until I show up. Period." He squeezes my shoulder. "Stick to the plan."

"Be careful," I warn.

"Yes, ma'am." He gives me a Boy Scout salute before heading out the door. I lock it behind him, uncomfortable being alone.

So I start digging around in the kitchen, searching for the rest of the canned goods.

Bavarian sauerkraut.

Okay. Not exactly an appetizing name.

I set the can aside and decide that I'll only be eating the contents if it's the *only* food I can find in the kitchen. Thankfully, I come across some cans of fruit and vegetables in one of the cupboards, sparing me the misery of eating the sauerkraut. I eat it cold, feeling a rush of energy come with the sugar.

The day is long and boring. I've got nobody to talk to besides myself - which makes me feel like I've gone crazy- so I resort to reading the books lying around the home. Whoever lived here had terribly dull taste in books. Nothing but poetry collections reminiscing unrequited love and a box of Reader's Digest. Inspirational stuff.

I end up taking a nap through the afternoon. I guess I'm more tired than I thought. By the time evening rolls around, I'm antsy, bored. Uncomfortable by myself.

It's sucks to be a survivor of an EMP. There's nothing to *do.*

"This is riveting," I mutter, flicking a crumb across the kitchen table.

But when nighttime comes, I start to get worried. *Tick, tock.* My mental clock is ticking – loudly. Chris said he'd be back by nighttime. With dinner. I pace the living room a few times, playing with my knife, fiddling with the ends of my hair. Reading poetry again. Cleaning the living room window with a rag.

At around eight o'clock, Chris still hasn't returned. I'm not *worried* in the normal sense. More like *concerned.* Maybe he got hurt and it's taking him a long time to limp back to the trailer. Maybe he ran into a gang. Maybe there was nothing to hunt so he decided to travel farther away from the trailer park to find food.

All possible scenarios. All things I imagine to keep myself from panicking.

Another hour drags by.

I throw on my boots.

Twenty minutes.

I put on my jacket.

Fifteen minutes.

I grab my knife and strap it to my thigh.

Five minutes.

I open the front door.

There's no light coming from inside the trailer, other than the tea lights I lit on the kitchen counters. I take a cautious step into the cool night air, clicking the door shut behind me. The sky is shrouded with rainclouds, making it difficult to navigate the trailer park without moonlight. I swallow a nervous lump in my throat before walking. I'm not really looking for Chris. I'm not going to find him. I just feel cooped up...and yeah. I'm *worried.*

I walk around the outer fence of the park, studying the melancholy appearance of the abandoned houses. Everything from children's toys to spare tires are scattered around the front lawns. Grass is growing around one tricycle, twisting through the tires.

Very. Creepy.

"You stay here and wait until I show up. Period," Chris said.

I wince, feeling guilty for leaving the trailer. I should go back. So I turn on my heel and head back to the trailer, making up my mind to sit and wait this one out. I've been through too much to run outside and get into trouble. I know better.

I've seen the dark side of society on more than one occasion.

I will do as I'm told.

When I reach our trailer, I open the door and slip inside. Chris hasn't returned. I sink into the sofa and sigh, attempting to relax.

*Chris will come back. He **always** comes back.*

And *bam*. Just like that, everything changes. It happens so quickly that I don't even have time to scream. The picture window at the front of the living room shatters. The glass simply *explodes*, coinciding with a piercing shriek near my head. I roll to the ground, instinctively covering my head with my hands. Shards of glass cut through my jacket, stinging the skin of my fingers.

What the...?

Silence.

I look up, head spinning, pushing off the floor with my hands. I wince as glass digs into my palms, drawing blood. Another pop rips the air and the lamp on the coffee table shatters. I snap my gaze to the kitchen, instantly finding the source of the problem: a gun. And a man holding it.

He's wearing a dark blue uniform. A white O is clearly visible on his shoulder sleeve.

Omega.

I freeze. Terror momentarily roots me to the spot. This is exactly what I've been scared of for *weeks.* Being found. And now I'm staring straight into the face of an Omega soldier, his gun trained at my head. He's apparently just as stunned as I am to make eye contact – and I'm even *more* stunned that he shot at me twice and *missed.*

Strangely enough, my first thought is:

Chris would never miss.

The guy snaps out of it, raising his weapon again. No dice. I turn on my heel and sprint outside, running as fast as I can. I weave between trailers, fueled with the strength and stamina of adrenaline.

I should be dead. That trooper *should* have nailed me.

God, what if he was already in the house *before* I left the trailer? I could have been killed sitting at the kitchen table.

Those kinds of thoughts only make me run faster. I skid around a corner and spot another guy in uniform, barely visible in the darkness, his head bobbing in my direction. He yells something along the lines of, "HALT!" I ignore the suggestion.

I turn and run the other way, rounding another corner, finding two more guards.

What is this? An ambush? How did they find us?

WHERE IS CHRIS?

I dart frantically across dead lawns, through backyards, underneath picnic tables and between flowerbeds. I hear footsteps and voices now, sounds that are getting closer as they pursue me. I run to the edge of the trailer park, eyeing one of the breaks in the chain link fence. I need to lose these suckers in the woods, but I can't bring myself to step away from the trailer park without Chris. He's tactically brilliant, and I can't see him stumbling into the lap of an Omega soldier. Maybe that's why he's not here yet.

Maybe he ran into a patrol, too.

"Chris!" I shout. I'm already being chased, so it's not like I'm giving myself away. "Christopher!"

Yeah, that's it. Go for the full name.

A stray shot whizzes by my ear, nearly grazing my cheek. I jerk backwards and head towards the fence, Omega soldiers flooding out of the trailer park like roaches. I can't believe how *many* there are. How could this happen? How long have they been tracking us?

I stop trying to rationalize the situation and slip through the break in the fence, diving into the woods. An eerie sense of Dejavu overwhelms me, taking me back to a couple of months ago when I was running from Omega in the mountains...

In the end, I'd escaped alive. Why not now?

I know without looking over my shoulder that I'm being chased by at least four people.

At *least.*

My advantage over them is that I'm small and lightening quick where they're burdened down with bulletproof vests and heavy weapons. So I press harder, sprinting through the undergrowth, putting more and more distance between the trailer park and me.

Just as I'm looking for place to hide, a jolting, electrifying pain spikes up my right leg. I'm running full speed when it happens, making me go down fast and hard. I tumble head over heels to the bottom of a small embankment covered with gravel. I cry out, looking at my ankle. I've been hit with...*something*. The dark material is wet with blood, hot and sticky against my skin.

I hobble to my feet and try to stand, only to get another electric jolt up my leg, straight to my chest. I gasp and fall to my knees, pulling the pant leg up. Something's been shot into my skin. A bullet? No. My leg would be broken. I crawl forward, trying to pull myself to my feet, but every time I put pressure on my leg, excruciating pain sends me straight back to the ground.

Ensconced in pain, I realize absently that the Omega soldiers are closing in. I hear their voices and make out their figures but it's nothing but background noise. This thing in my leg is *killing* me. It's my point of focus.

When an Omega man closes his hand around my arm, I a sense of clarity returns and I jam my elbow into his chest. He lets go and I hit the ground with an unattractive *thud*. Before I can scramble to my feet I hear one thing and feel another.

I hear: *Put her down.*

And then I *feel* a tremendous blow to the side of my head, making the pain disappear.

Everything goes black.

Not the highlight of my day.

Chapter Three

Growing up, I always had very vivid dreams. I rarely had a dream that revolved around the imaginary – everything I dreamed about was related to real life. My mom, my dad, my homework. Whatever was in my head before I fell asleep was the subject of my dreams.

Today is no different, except for the fact that I'm not asleep. I'm unconscious. *How* I became unconscious I have no idea, but I have a feeling it's not good. I'm stuck in an in-between world of dreaming and reality, mixing real sights and sounds with my imagination. Bursts of light, deep voices, soreness in my leg...*what happened to my leg, anyway? What happened to Chris? Where am I...and why can't I wake up?*

I try to shake myself awake. It doesn't work. I'm stuck in darkness. No feeling, no nothing. I can only hope that I'm not dead and that this isn't some kind of lame version of heaven.

"Wake. Up."

I bob to the surface of reality. The same voice repeats the words again. And again. It gets more and more irritated.

It ticks me off.

I'm *trying* to wake up. Don't rush me.

Light slips into the darkness, and with it, *feeling.* I feel cold. I feel thirsty. I feel like I need a hot shower.

Yeah. *That's* my first thought when my eyes open and I find myself staring at a gray ceiling.

"Finally. Geez, it took you long enough."

As I focus on the scenery around me, I realize for the first time that my head is crammed against a wall. And I'm moving. Well, *bouncing* would be a more accurate term. A figure is crouched at my feet. She's got dark skin, short brown hair and glittering hazel eyes.

"You're not very polite," she states.

I sit up, dizzy, and look around. Someone's ankle is pressing against the back of my head.

Wait.

What?

I jerk upright, overwhelmed by the stench of human sweat. It's beyond disgusting. I'm crushed against the back wall of a of truck, and everywhere around me, people are standing next to each other, packed tightly together.

Sardines in a can.

"What? I don't...who...?" I stutter. I'm disoriented, terrified, sick. Confused. "What's going *on*?"

No one pays me any attention. I can't move, because I'm stuck between too many people. The air is humid and difficult to inhale. It reeks of vomit and urine. I gag and roll to my side, crawling on hands and knees.

"Where do you think you're going?" the girl asks.

I turn back to face her. I'd forgotten she was here.

"Who are you?" I ask, trembling.

It's hot. The only cool air is coming from above the heads of the standing crowd, so I try to get to my feet. When I do, I fall over and hit the ground.

Graceful.

The back of the truck is open. We're fenced in behind a metal mesh gate. Chicken wire? Perhaps. It's dark outside, and I can't make out anything beyond flashes of trees.

"Sophia," she says. The girl is crouched in a feral position, studying my face. "My name is *Sophia.* What's yours?"

"My...name?" I clutch the floor. "Um...right. My name." I meet Sophia's gaze. She's surprisingly calm. Considering the fact that we're crammed into the back of a giant semi truck, I'm impressed. "I'm Cassidy."

"Nice to meet you." She crawls closer and takes my hand. "Don't worry. It's okay to be scared, sometimes."

"What's going on?' I whisper.

"Omega is taking us to prison," she shrugs. "Or something like that."

"I don't remember how I got here," I say. "I was running. I got shot."

"No, not shot," Sophia replies. "Just shocked, plus you got hit on the head. You're okay. But you were delirious when they shoved you back here. I made sure you didn't get squished when they crammed everybody inside."

I stare at her, rubbing the sore spot on my temple.

"Why?"

She looks down. "You looked like you needed somebody to help you."

My eyes sting.

Someone helped me. Because they could.

"Thank you," I say.

She flashes an embarrassed smile.

"No problem." She huddles closer. "Where did they pick you up?"

"I was in a trailer park," I reply, biting my lip. "They must have had a patrol in the area. They probably saw me walking around outside. Stupid *me*. I should have stayed *inside* like he said!"

"Like who said?"

"My…" I trail off. "Chris. He's going to be mad when he finds out I'm missing."

That's an understatement. As the reality of my situation sinks in, I fight to remain calm. I've been caught by Omega. I'm crammed in the back of a semi-truck with a thousand other people. We're being taken to prison – or something along those lines – and the chances of me living to see the light of day are slim.

I fold my arms around my chest and take deep, slow breaths. It doesn't help. There isn't a Zen zone on this side of the planet that could calm me down. I'm being shipped off to my death.

And everybody in this truck knows it.

"I'm from New York," Sophia whispers, scooting close to me. "I was on vacation in California when the EMP hit. My family is still in New York somewhere."

Her eyes shine with tears. Tears I sympathize with.

"I heard our military is fighting somewhere on the East Coast," I reply.

A woman shifts and kicks me in the ribs. I pull away and huddle towards the wall, Sophia right beside me. I keep my eyes closed to avoid looking at the sickening rocking motion of the truck.

"Yes," Sophia answers. "I've heard that. I've also heard that it's a lot worse on the East Coast than it is over here."

"Why?"

"They say it's an active battle zone right now."

What's left of the color in my face drains away.

"What kind of a battle zone?" I ask.

"Don't know. By the time news gets here, it's all nothing but rumors." She sighs. "Could be nuclear war. Maybe. But I've heard that Omega's actually got a huge front of troops moving in over there."

Yeah. The sick feeling I just had?

It's back.

"You can't be serious," I mutter. But I know she is. And deep down, I knew something big was going down on the East Coast. I just didn't know what.

We still don't, but that gives me more of an idea.

"Where do these people come from?" I say.

"I heard-" Sophia begins, but closes her mouth. "I'll tell you later."

Several of the prisoners in the truck are listening to our conversation a little *too* closely. And by the way they're dressed – not to mention the way they *smell* – I'm guessing they've had a worse day than me.

"Where are they taking us?" I ask instead.

"Don't know. Did they pick you up in Squaw Valley?"

"Yeah. You?"

"Same. I was with a community, though. What's left of the city was living in a neighborhood just off the road. Omega came, rounded us up, threw us in a truck and now we're here." She clenches her fists. "They're not looking for people to kill anymore."

"Then what are we here for?"

Sophia's eyes narrow.

"To work."

I don't get a warm and fuzzy feeling from *that* statement either.

Keep it together.

I think about Chris and *only* Chris.

What is he doing right now? He'll discover that I'm gone when he comes back from his hunting expedition. He'll be angry. He'll think I went looking for him. And then he'll start searching for me. But how will he be able to track a truck? How will be ever find me?

He won't, a little voice says. Its name is common sense. *You're on your own.*

No way. I'm not alone. Chris will find me.

Even if he ***does*** *find you, you'll be dead by the time he does.*

I shudder. Common sense is stupid.

All through the night, the truck keeps moving. When the soft glow of morning hits the opening at the end of the trailer, I strain to see where we are. I can't see outside, though. Not with the enormous amount of arms and legs blocking my view. Sophia falls asleep on my shoulder. I'm too exhausted to shake her off, and besides. The girl *did* take care of me when I was unconscious. The least I can do is allow her to rest undisturbed.

And then we stop.

I freeze. Doors slam. Men's voices echo outside the trailer. The rumble of nearby engines. Sophia snaps awake beside me. She grabs my arm, scared.

"We must be here."

There's movement at the end of the trailer. I wobble to my feet, wincing with the pressure. My ankle is still sore from being hit with a stun gun, I guess. Unsurprising. There's a hushed murmur right before the crowd surges forward. It's so sudden that Sophia and I are smashed together. I can't breathe. Somebody at the entrance of the trailer yells, "EVERYBODY OUT!"

We're dragged out of the truck along with the other prisoners. When we reach the mouth of the exit, I'm blinded by the sun. It's unnaturally bright compared to the darkness of the truck. A guard grabs my arm and throws me to the ground. I land in a heap, scraping my hands on dirt.Sophia slams into my back. She gets to her feet, grimacing.

"Sorry," she breathes.

I look around, attempting to get my bearings. We're on a dirt road, and all around us are rows of perfectly aligned fruit trees. Oranges, by the looks of it. An irrigation canal is running alongside the road. I get a good look at the truck: A semi with a fruit packing-shed insignia on the side.

Oh, my God.

They've been commandeered.

Omega guards in dark blue uniforms surround the truck, literally throwing people to the ground.

"Come on, line up. Move it." An Omega trooper with thick black hair and pale skin shoves his gun into my back. I scramble to my feet. Sophia clutches my arm. We're pushed into a group of prisoners. As we round the side of the truck, my jaw drops. Three trucks are parked in front of us, all of them packed with more prisoners. About fifty yards down the road is a huge complex of buildings. The structure is gray with dark orange roofing. A makeshift fence has been erected around the property, topped off with coils of barbed wire.

This isn't your average prison.

"Move it, go forward. Come on."

The same pale guard brings up the rear of this group, and I notice something else. Our truckload is made up of female prisoners. There aren't any men in our group, although I can see a gathering of male prisoners farther down the road. They're keeping us separated, which is the only positive thing that I can see about this situation.

"Do you know where we are?" Sophia whispers.

The two of us are linked arm in arm, afraid of being separated. We've only known each other for a couple of hours, but already we've latched onto an important survival instinct: stick together. It might be the only thing that keeps us alive.

"No, but..." I trail off as we approach the fence. Guards are standing at the gate, watching the prisoners arrive. The complex is surrounded with concrete. An asphalt road curves around the property. A sign marked **School Crossing** is leaning sideways over the pavement. That's when it hits me. This is – *was* – a school.

The name of the school has been ripped off the front of the building. In its place is a rough outline of where the letters used to be. I feel chilled. To the bone.

Sophia shudders.

"I can't believe this," she bites out.

"I can."

In fact, I expect it of them.

I shut my mouth as the pale guard comes up beside us. When we pass through the front entrance, I experience a sudden rush of desperation.

Out of the frying pan and into the fire.

As soon as I step onto the sidewalk, my heart sinks.

We're *inside*, now.

Getting out is going to be difficult, if not impossible. Outdoor halls, offices, administrative buildings, classrooms and a gymnasium dot the property. Everything was once well watered and green. Flowers had been planted in front of the main office. Now everything is dead. Yellow. Sections of the school have been separated with cheap but effective fencing, making the entire complex one big series of inescapable walls.

If you get past one wall, you just have to get past another one.

Nice.

Our group is led down a long outdoor hallway, heading towards the gym. It's like high school all over again, I swear. I always hated P.E. Cruel irony.

The front doors are propped open. Vending machines sit empty near the walls. We step inside the gym, and I'm immediately hit with the same stench I had to put up with in the truck. Sweat. Vomit. Other unmentionable scents better left unsaid.

The gym is crawling with prisoners. They're being herded into different rows. Omega officers are crowding men and women into separate locker rooms. I get a fleeting glance at the empty bleachers. A blue and gold banner is tacked above the backboard of the basketball court:

GO TIGERS! FIGHT!

If only.

Sophia and I squeeze into a single file line. She stands in front. I follow. The pale guard with the black hair – I'm going to call him Grease, because it looks like his hair hasn't been washed in a while – gives me a long, unsettling look before heading off to join the men's group. He's replaced by a score of female Omega guards arriving from the locker room. They're fair-skinned, dark haired women with loud voices. One woman in particular catches my eye as she walks to the front of the line. Her hair is pulled back so tightly that it looks as if her skin might tear apart.

A small nametag catches the light on her breast pocket:

V. Kameneva.

Russian.

She notices my stare at her and flicks her laser gaze at me. I flinch and instinctively look away.

My cheeks warm and I stare at the ground, praying that she won't speak to me. She doesn't, but she throws several glances in my direction as I pass. Because of her nametag and the red band tied around her left arm, I make the assumption that she's an officer rather than a mere soldier. She's overseeing the arrival of new prisoners.

"Cassidy," Sophia hisses, stiffening.

"What?"

I peek around her, watching the line of people disappearing into the girls' locker room. As we're pushed inside, we're crammed between rows of lockers. Everything from candy wrappers to musty bathroom towels are scattered across the floor. I'm guessing when the EMP hit, this school evacuated fast. Maybe they were in the middle of a basketball game when it all went down...

Flecks of cold water hit my face, and I get a glimpse of what's going on down the line. The showers are running at full blast. The privacy curtains have been torn off. Women are being forced to strip and walk through the showers.

"How do they get the plumbing to work?" Sophia whispers.

"They must have their own generators," I reply. "Maybe they're tapped into a private well or something."

"Strip down and leave your clothes at your feet!" The woman named V. Kamaneva marches down the aisle, gesturing to the showers. "Walk through the showers quickly.

You will be inspected and then you will be given new clothes. Move it along quickly! No delays!"

I'm momentarily frozen. Embarrassment, shock and a thousand other emotions rush through my system, and before I know it, I'm standing at the front of the line, right next to Sophia. We're both terrified.

Sophia looks like she's going to pass out. I might, too.

Kamaneva claps her hands together in front of my face. "You're holding up the line! Move it, move it!"

The armed female guards in the corner of the room look bored with what's going on. I stare at the floor and strip off my clothes – even my beloved combat boots. When I'm done, I realize that the only thing I haven't removed is the necklace that Chris gave me months ago. His graduation necklace.

Panicked at the thought of losing it, I remove it from my neck and pretend to set it inside my pile of clothes. With all the noise and commotion – not to mention the absolute humiliation of being forced to march naked through a row of showers – I pop it into my mouth.

The gold tastes sour against my tongue.

Sophia and I walk through the showers. The water is *freezing*. The pressure is powerful. Painful, even.

When we finally finish the shower run, we stumble to the other side of the locker room. More female Omega troopers are waiting. Half of them are armed. The other half is standing there, chucking towels in our faces. I catch one. It's covered in dirt and grime. Lovely. I wipe the water off my body, attempting to dry my hair.

On the bright side, I'm clean.

On the not-so-bright-side, I'm naked.

I keep my eyes glued to the wall or the ground. I can't look at the other women here. I'm embarrassed, humiliated.

Mortified.

After the bulk of the prisoners have dried off, Omega guards throw clothes in our faces. I grab the material. It's rough, brown and ugly. The fashion police would shoot me on sight if I walked around in this thing in Los Angeles. But it's something to *wear*, so I throw it on. It's a shapeless piece of cloth, little better than a potato sack. A basic set of trousers with nothing more than a piece of string to keep them around my waist. That, supplemented with a dirty tee shirt, completes our uniforms.

Sophia gives me a once over when we get the clothes on.

"Pretty bad," she mouths.

I almost smile.

They give us shoes. They're all piled into different sizes, as if someone fished them out of a dumpster. I get stuck with a pair of cheap gladiator flip-flops that are two sizes two big.

These won't last more than a day.

Kamaneva and her guards throw open the rear-exit to the locker room.

"This way. Get in line!"

We move again. At the door, two female guards are waiting with scissors. I blanch. They're cutting hair. *Our* hair. I grab my long, curly, red locks, hair that falls to my waist. Hair that I've been growing out since I was in Middle School. Sophia stands motionless in the doorway. Her hair is already above her shoulders, therefore they only end up cutting off a few inches. Just enough to make it a generic, masculine hairstyle.

I've still got Chris's necklace between my teeth, so I keep my mouth closed. But I'm nothing short of horrified. Take away my clothes and dignity, but don't cut off my hair. Ever. The woman with the scissors holds my wet hair in her hand studies it. I swear she almost looks sorry.

Almost.

I hear the *snip* of the scissors. My head feels like it's floating above my shoulders. The weight is gone. I touch my scalp. My hair is probably only a few inches long. Long enough to be combed over, but not long enough to put in a ponytail.

I spit the necklace into my hand and tie it onto the inside of my shirt. And then I begin to cry silently, shocked with the loss of my long hair, humiliated from marching naked through a hall of showers, sick from being hauled in a semi-truck as if I were a piece of livestock.

It's like a tornado of bad luck. A hurricane.

A blizzard.

Sophia stops me. She takes my face between her hands and grits out, "Stop crying. We're not safe yet." She gives my shoulders a rough shake. "Cassidy? Come on. We'll get through this together."

I take a deep breath, barely able to see her through my tears. Sophia nods and hooks her arm through mine, and then we're moving *again.*

There's really no downtime around this place, is there?

We're led away from the gymnasium, back towards the center of the school. Towards the classrooms. I see a science building, a history building…I sigh. History was always my favorite subject growing up. Why does Omega have to take anything that's halfway decent and turn it into something twisted?

Kamaneva and her guards open up another set of doors.

We're marched inside a classroom marked *LAB*. Chairs, desks, books, pencils and anything else of remote convenience have been removed from the room. All that remains are plain counters, minus the vials and test tubes. The only windows are small slits near the top of the ceiling, making an escape through those openings impossible.

Kamaneva walks to a chalkboard at the front of the room. She grabs a piece of chalk from the lip at the bottom of the board – I'd like to know who left *chalk* in the room but took everything else – and starts writing. Nobody dares say a word. There are about thirty or forty of us packed inside the room.

She writes:

Group 13.

"*You* are Group 13," she states, turning to face us. She folds her hands behind her back, a cold expression on her face. "When you hear your number, you respond immediately. If we call Group 13 out in the morning, you come *right away.* If you disobey regulations, your *entire* group will be punished."

"What are the regulations?" someone asks.

I keep my eyes trained on Kamaneva. She draws her hands to her sides, annoyed.

"Regulation Number One," she says, taking a commanding tone. "You do not speak unless you are addressed *first* or asked a direct question." Burn. "Regulation Number Two, you do not make a move without direct orders to do so. This includes, eating, sleeping, walking, talking, moving, working and *thinking*."

"Inspirational speaker," I whisper.

Sophia slaps my hand.

I guess my sense of sarcasm is returning.

"Regulation Number Three," she continues. "No prisoner at any time is to *ever* carry a weapon. If you are found in possession of a weapon, you will be executed immediately." She pauses. "Regulation Number Four, obey all of the above regulations, or you'll be killed. Are we clear?"

No one says anything.

What can you say to something like that, anyway?

She gives a brief nod, walks towards the door, and *bam*. We're moving. No more than five minutes of peace. We're walking back out the doors, away from the chemistry lab, and I've got a bad feeling about where this whacked out tour is headed.

We're rounded through more double doors and enter a huge room filled with plastic tables and chairs. Omega guards are posted at every corner. A group of twenty male prisoners are huddled around tables, eating.

"This is where you will eat your meals," Kamaneva announces. "You will get two: breakfast and dinner. You will never take more than the portion given to you. Stealing food will result in severe punishment." Her lips curl up at the corners. "You'll have ten minutes every morning to eat. Ten minutes at night." She makes a motion and the guards fall into place around us, goading us outside again. "While you are here you will move quickly and learn to anticipate orders."

We reach the outside of the school, where the orange groves are growing in abundance. The bushy green trees are overgrown, aligned in perfect rows. Oranges are hanging heavy on the branches. They're ready to be picked. Outside of the orange groves are several empty fields, and down from that, more oranges.

"Group 13," she says. "Your job will be harvesting the fruit that is already on the trees. When you are done, you will move on to planting."

I share a glance with Sophia.

Really?

Omega brought us all the way out here to *farm*?

Male Omega troopers move in and surround us. A couple of pickup trucks covered in mud roll in, each of them hauling trailers. My jaw drops. It's been months since I've seen a working vehicle outside of Omega's designated military Humvees. This isn't possible. Not unless Omega was a lot more prepared for an EMP than we were. In that case, I can think of several theories...

But not right now.

Troops are popping open the trailers. Ladders, sacks and boxes are packed into the bed. Kamaneva points to the trucks. "You will harvest the entire orange crop," she announces. "Fill your sacks, bring them back to this point, then place them in boxes. You will have water periodically, when troops provide it. You start today. There's no introductory period. Go."

Just like that. I have a job.

Unemployment has officially ended.

Sophia and I stay close to each other, moving towards one of the pickup trucks. The early morning sunlight breaks over the horizon, illuminating the distant Sierra Nevada Mountain Range. I can see Mt. Whitney sparkling with snow from my vantage point on the ground. It must be nice to be unmoving and unaffected by everything around you. To stand for thousands of years and stay the same.

I'd like to be a mountain.

Then again, I'd also like to eat at McDonald's.

Welcome to my world.

"You."

Sophia and I come to a halt. Kamaneva is standing a few feet behind us, her hands clasped in front of her. Up close, I notice the wrinkles around her eyes. The frown lines around her mouth. She's older than I thought.

"You're friends?" she asks.

I manage to shake my head.

"Hmm." She steps closer, placing one finger under our chins. "I had two daughters, once. They were young like the both of you."

I keep my expression neutral.

It's a challenge.

"One of them died," she goes on. "The other one lived."

She removes her fingers and steps back.

"It would be such a pity if you found yourselves in the same situation."

She gives us a long, hard look before turning and stalking off. Sophia stares after her.

"What the hell was that supposed to mean?" she whispers.

I lick my lips.

"I don't know," I say.

"Hey, you two! Get to work!"

Grease the guard is back. He throws two cloth sacks at our feet. Sophia and I bend to pick them up, slipping the thick strap over our shoulders. Some of the other women are hauling heavy ladders into the field. Omega guards are barking orders. Everyone is tense, afraid to ask questions, afraid to defy the instructions.

We're terrified.

It would be such a pity if you found yourselves in the same situation.

Who is V. Kamaneva? She comes across as strange and cruel. And I haven't even seen this woman in action yet. Sophia and I follow the other workers into the fields, Grease keeping close to us. "You pick the oranges, put them in the sack," he commands. Then he points to the end of the row of trees, where male prisoners are bringing out large boxes. "You put the oranges in there. Other workers will sort them. You don't worry about that. You just pick." To my surprise, he gives us a smile. A creepy, make-me-want-to-crawl-in-a-closet smile. Sophia pushes up next to me. "Is it just me or is he bad news?" she asks.

"He *is* bad news," I say. "And his hair is disgusting."

Hair.

Something I don't have a lot of anymore.

I take a deep breath, look up at the orange trees, and try to zone out. Think of something else. Something *other* than the fact that I've been forced into slave labor.

Like why Omega needs us to pick oranges.

"What's the point of this?" Sophia states as we walk towards a group of women placing a ladder against a tree. "How does picking oranges help Omega take over the world?"

"Well..." I lower my voice, conscious of the armed Omega men standing guard on the edges of the fields. "You said you thought something big was going down on the East Coast, right? Omega has a lot of troops over there."

"Right."

"You said it could have even been a nuclear war."

"Yeah, so...?"

"So Omega has got to be some kind of cover name. An organization that nobody's ever heard of doesn't just pop up out of the blue, nuke New York, hit the East Coast with a full frontal assault and then start taking over the country." I run a hand through my choppy hair. "Somebody big is behind this, and you and I aren't getting the full story because there's no way to *communicate* with people who really *do* know what's going on."

"Okay, but that doesn't answer the orange question," Sophia deadpans, raising an eyebrow. "World domination and fruit packing…? Come on."

"I'm guessing Omega needs food," I reply. "Look at it this way. If you're an invading army, you're going to need some way to feed your troops. If New York is really nuked, then it's possible that other places are too. Omega's going to need food. That would explain why they're bringing us here. They need us to harvest what's already here and then start planting new crops."

I hug my arms around my chest, surprised that I put the pieces together without Chris's help. He's always the one who explains Omega's evil intentions like a boss.

An Omega guard yells at us suddenly, telling us to quit standing around, working our jaws. It scares the crap out of us to get singled out of the entire group like that, so we climb up a ladder and start picking. I've never done this kind of work before, and at first, it seems easy enough. Pick an orange, put it in your sack, climb back down when it's full, and then dump the oranges in the bins for the male workers to haul away.

Until I do it over and over again. Without food and water. Without breaks. And without a place to use the restroom. It goes from easy to torturous in a snap.

"There really aren't very many troops in the Central Valley," Sophia says to me as we're hauling a huge sack of oranges to the end of the field. The sun is high in the sky, and we've been working for at least four hours. My arms are sore. My neck is sunburned, and despite the cold temperature, I'm soaked in sweat. "How much food can it take to feed a few soldiers?"

I drop my eyes to the white bins at the end of the field, making sure nobody can hear me. "Maybe they're getting ready."

"For *what*?"

"For backup."

Sophia's mouth forms a little O as we reach the bins, dump our oranges in, and head back to the trees. "If they're on the East Coast...maybe they're working their way closer?" Sophia suggests.

"No." I shake my head. "I don't think so. Something else is going on. But have you noticed how all of these troops are Russian? Soviet Union, anyone?"

"The Soviet Union did *not* invade the United States," Sophia says, smirking. "They don't exist anymore. Besides, it'd take a lot more than Russia, don't you think?"

"Right. They couldn't do it alone."

Isn't that the truth? Nobody could take over the world's greatest superpower without some serious firepower, some serious planning...and some serious big wheels backing them up. There's a lot more to Omega than meets the eye.

Not a concept I'm thrilled to realize.

Chapter Four

Omega is like an annoying relative that you can't get rid of. They're always there, waiting for you to make a mistake. Waiting for you to cross an invisible line. And when you *do* cross that line, you're dead.

Game over.

My first day at the labor camp is nothing short of miserable. I lose my hair, my clothes, my dignity and my independence. Something I *don't* lose is my appetite or my need to drink clean water. Hunger and thirst are the two things at the forefront of my mind as the hours pass.

Throughout the first day, Sophia and I work hard, picking oranges, putting them in our sacks, taking them to the bins. Rinse and repeat. It's very boring. Very tiring. We don't enjoy any downtime.

At around two in the afternoon, a pickup truck drives up to the corner of the field. Prisoners flood towards it. Sophia and I hang back, cautious. A huge plastic water tank sits on the back of the pickup bed. We approach slowly, watching while prisoners fill old milk cartons, thermoses and plastic water bottles. Sophia licks her lips.

"Where do we get some of those?" she says.

"I don't know."

Prisoners push and shove to the front of the line, filling their containers and gorging themselves with water. My dry mouth is *very* jealous right now.

"Hey." Grease marches up from the side of the field. He tosses a plastic milk carton at my chest. He gives an oversized orange juice can to Sophia. "You're welcome."

I open and close my mouth a few times before blurting out,

"Thank you."

But he's already gone.

"That's not right," Sophia observes. "He wants something from us."

"I don't care. I'm thirsty."

I work my way to the pickup bed and pull the lever on the container. Cold water comes rushing out. Probably ditchwater. Not long ago I would have rolled over and died before I drank out of a ditch. Today I don't care.

Funny how things have changed.

I fill the container to the brim and screw the lid tight just as I'm roughly shoved aside by a male prisoner. I hit the ground on my shoulder, wincing with pain. I get to my feet. My cheeks flush with anger and embarrassment. I feel like crying. Or kicking him. Maybe both. But no one even notices I was knocked down. I'm invisible. Sophia rushes up behind me and places her hand on my shoulder.

"You okay?" she whispers.

I nod.

"I'm going to get some water, too." She squeezes through the crowd, gets her own water, and the two of us head back to the trees. Away from the crazy prisoners pushing and clawing their way to the water.

"Next time we'll just go last," I say.

Sophia agrees, then we pop the lids off our cartons and drink. It's cold and refreshing, even if there *are* flecks of dirt and God-knows-what floating in the water. It does what it's supposed to do.

It keeps me alive.

"How long do you think our workday is?" Sophia wonders.

She climbs to the top of the ladder. I work my way up behind her, swinging onto the trunk of the tree. After just a few hours of working out here, we've already got a system down. She picks produce at the top of the ladder, because she's taller, and I bend down and get the oranges underneath the canopy of branches that she would have a hard time reaching. "Probably from sunrise to sunset," I sigh. "And I'm doubting we get a dental plan."

Sophia snorts.

"I'm doubting we get *anything*."

"I wonder when we eat." I drop a couple of oranges into my bag. "Kamaneva said we get ten minutes for dinner."

"Ten minutes? That's not enough. I need an hour. At least."

"An *hour*? It doesn't take that long to eat."

"You've never met my family."

I grin for the first time since arriving.

The rest of the day passes slowly, and the by the time evening hits, I'm exhausted – mentally and physically. Every once in a while Sophia and I will hear the boom and rattle of distant gunfire, reminding us that we're working in the midst of an active warzone. It's chilling.

"Hey, listen." Sophia pauses, cocking her head. "What's that?"

I stop. The school intercom is emitting a piercing tone. It sounds like a heart rate monitor that's flat-lined. All around us, seasoned prisoners stop what they're doing, grab their ladders, and take off.

"I'm guessing we're done," I say.

Sophia takes one end of the ladder and I take the other. We haul it to the end of the field and heave it into the back of a pickup. We grab our water containers and watch as other prisoners drop their shoulder sacks into a bin. Sophia and I follow suit and blend into the crowd as armed Omega troopers close in around us. It's not long before we're moving back into the complex. We march down the long corridors before making a sharp turn into the cafeteria.

Sophia and I are clueless about how to proceed, so we let the other prisoners surge in front of us while we bring up the rear. They line up at a long, low table. Stacks of bowls are piled at one end. All of the prisoners grab one.

"I have a bad feeling about this," I say.

I take a bowl and file down the side of the table. I hold my bowl out as a woman – a fellow prisoner, by the looks of it - spoons something hot and steaming into the container. I stare at the contents. It looks like muddy water.

"What *is* this?" Sophia hisses.

"I don't think I want to know." We're given a piece of hard bread at the end of the line and Sophia and I sit down at a plastic table in the corner. "This bread is ancient." I try to break it in half, but it's too stale. It won't even bend. "My teeth are screwed."

"It's better than nothing," Sophia says. "...I think."

The mystery soup is little more than water with a few spices, some chunks of unidentifiable meat and a dash flour thrown in. I soak the bread in the bowl to get it soft enough to eat. Honestly, I've had better meals. Then again, I've had worse meals. I *did* live in Los Angeles, after all. The dining experiences there can be hit and miss. I went through a lot of trial and error in high school to find the restaurants that were worth the time and money.

This is not worth time or money. Or caloric value.

I don't see a rosy, healthy future for myself if this is the only food we get. It's basically thickened gruel and a piece of stale bread. It's not enough to keep an anorexic canary alive, let alone a human being.

Maybe we'll get more food tomorrow.

Keep dreaming, my little voice says.

In the end, Kamaneva is right. We only get ten minutes to eat, which is more than enough time considering the fact that our meal has less mass than bottled baby food. Afterwards we're marched back to the *LAB*. The doors are shut behind us and locked tight. Armed Omega troopers are stationed in the hall and outside the windows.

Sophia and I press our backs against the far wall and drop to the ground, watching other prisoners crawl into their own spaces. Some squeeze underneath the lab counters and curl up inside the big storage cupboards. Others literally sprawl out wherever they are and close their eyes. Arms and legs are everywhere, and the women don't seem to be embarrassed to prop their legs up on each other's backs or stick their head in somebody's face.

I, on the other hand, *am* embarrassed. I lean my head against the wall and close my eyes. I'm too stressed to analyze anything. I'm too exhausted to think about the fact that just last night, I was searching for Chris at the trailer park.

Just last night I was still a free person.

"Goodnight, Cassidy," Sophia yawns.

"Night."

I fall asleep.

I'm too tired to do anything else.

Whether or not it's normal, everyone tends to fall into a routine. Even if you're a prisoner at a slave labor camp, picking oranges and being bossed around by a Russian soldier with a long, confusing name. That's what happens to me: I get familiar with the routine at camp. Our schedule is simple, so it's not hard to do:

1. Get up at sunrise. Eat breakfast. Ten minutes.
2. Get to work. Harvest the orange trees. This could go on forever. The fields are endlessly huge.
3. Sunset. Eat dinner. Ten minutes.
4. Head to our cellblocks, also known as *LAB*. Group 13 shuts down and rests for the day.

We never deviate from our schedule. There's never any change, and despite the high stress environment and the fact that, hey, we're *enslaved*, I actually get used to the lifestyle here. Hard, grueling work. Borderline starvation. Bullying, taunting and humiliation from the soldiers. It's not a pretty picture. But that's the beauty of being human, right? We adapt to even the most difficult situations. Plus, I'm smaller than some of the other prisoners, so the paltry amount of nutrition we receive here goes farther with me. Big, muscular men quickly become weak and emaciated, but smaller people like me? We last a little longer.

Well, for the most part.

I can't stop worrying about Chris.

What is doing right now? Is he looking for me? Or did he give up on ever finding me again? I wouldn't blame him. How would he track a truck all the way to...wherever I am? Somewhere in the Central Valley.

And what about Dad? What's happening to him? Was he captured and taken to an Omega facility just like this? Is this what happened to Chris's family? How am I ever supposed to *find* them if I'm stuck in prison?

The frustration is a physical force.

It's one thing to be separated from the people you love. It's another thing to be separated by bars, barbed wire and armed guards. It's a nightmare. But Sophia helps me keep it together. We complement each other well. She's calm where I'm angry, and I'm strong where she's weak.

"You know what's ironic?" she asks me.

We're in a new field of oranges, and we're harvesting as fast as we can. The temperature has risen and the fruit is ripening quicker. Omega wants everything taken off the trees *pronto,* so they can feed their men. But oranges aren't exactly the kind of food you give an army.

Unless the army is desperate for anything they can find...and they're just taking what's here before they start planting what *they* want. The question is, what *do* they want, and who are they feeding? Because there aren't enough troops in the Central Valley of California alone to warrant a production like this.

Right?

"Hello?" Sophia waves a hand in front of my face.

"Hmm? Oh, sorry." I shrug. "I was thinking."

"Obviously." She wipes the sweat off her forehead. Already I can see the effects of severe hunger on her face. Sharper cheekbones, a more angular jawline. I'm betting that if I could see myself in a mirror, I'd notice some not-so-attractive changes in my own face, too. "I said, isn't it ironic that the only reason Omega needs us to do all this is because of the EMP?"

I blink.

"What do you mean?"

"I mean *all of this.* Omega needs labor because they destroyed the infrastructure of the country with an EMP." She holds an orange in front of my face. "They created their own problem and they're having us solve it for them. It's not fair!"

"Of course it's not." I stifle a cough into my hand. "Omega's got this place pretty well organized, though. Everybody's got a job. They're using us to our full potential. It's transporting and storing the food we're harvesting that's got to be hard for them, I guess. "

"What do you mean, *I guess*?" She smirks.

"Well...you're assuming that Omega is behind the EMP."

"Of *course* they are. Who else would be?"

I look around for any overly curious listeners. Talking amongst ourselves while working is against the rules, so we try to keep chitchat to a minimum.

"Think about it," I whisper. "These troops are Russian. A few months ago I saw international troops in Bakersfield speaking German. There was an officer that captured Chris and me. His name was Keller. He was *very* not Russian, and he definitely wasn't American."

"So what are you saying? Omega is culturally diverse?"

"Yes." I make a move to pull my hair over my shoulder, and then stop. There *is* no hair to pull. My hands swish through empty space. "Russia, Europe...Omega isn't just one conglomerate that came out of nowhere. It's something a bunch of people...maybe a bunch of *countries* are calling themselves to create chaos. Keep us in the dark. If we don't know who's attacking us, it's kind of hard to know who to fight, don't you think? We don't have TV or radio to communicate with each other. Everyone's scared and confused, and in comes a bunch of people calling themselves Omega. It's strategically brilliant."

"So you think Omega is an alliance of countries?"

I open my mouth to respond, but I'm interrupted by a harsh,

"Of course that's what Omega is."

I whip around, almost bumping into a tall young man with curly brown hair. The first thing I notice about him are his piercing blue eyes.

Piercing.

"You're not supposed to be here," I snap. "This is Group 13's area."

"I was sent here by my Group Leader," he replies. He's got a British accent. It suits him. "Apparently you're not working fast enough."

I peek over his shoulder. He's right. Male workers are moving into the field with sacks. Some of the women look downright terrified to see male prisoners, and I don't blame them. Sophia and I have had a couple of ugly run-ins with men in the prison that have lost all sense of dignity and morality. Making sure the sexes are separated is the only thing that keeps this labor camp moving. Omega must be hungry or they wouldn't let us work together.

This is the first sign of weakness I've seen from them.

"Omega *is* an alliance," the young man says, following us. "You're dead on about that."

"Look, we probably shouldn't be talking," Sophia replies, nervous.

"I've been here for three months," the man answers, cracking a smile. "Trust me, if you keep your voices down and close your mouth when the guards walk by, you'll be fine."

I climb the ladder and crane my neck to see how many oranges we've got left. After five days, I'm sick of seeing oranges. Outright *sick.*

"Okay then," I say, careful. "What do you know about Omega?"

"Well," he replies, "I know what you know. But I've heard different rumors, so I have a slightly different theory."

"Do tell," Sophia says, folding her arms across her chest.

"Omega is like an umbrella," he explains. "Underneath it are several different forces working together, but only one of those forces are responsible for the EMP. You know that an EMP is caused by a nuclear explosion in the atmosphere, yes?"

We nod.

"You have to ask yourself, who in the world today has the firepower and the gall to do something like that to the United States?" he pauses. "I'm from London, but I was living in Hollywood when the EMP struck. Omega is probably an alliance of countries, and one of those countries sent out the nuclear blast that destroyed our technology."

"That's kind of what I was already saying," I deadpan. "Just...with a little more detail."

He chuckles.

"I'm Harry, by the way," he says. "Harry Lydell, but who cares about your last name these days, right? Who are you?"

"I'm Cassidy and this is Sophia," I reply. "Welcome to the club."

"Club?"

"Yeah. Our club." Sophia and I share a secret grin.

Harry looks confused, but he doesn't question us. He ends up being a good worker. Fast, quiet, observant. Smart. The guy has some interesting theories about Omega and the source of the EMP, which makes my curious ears perk up. Anything is more interesting than manual labor, anyway. And to be honest, I'm glad to have somebody else to talk to. It's been just Sophia and me since we were smashed together in the semi-truck, and it's nice to have a newbie to get to know.

The three of us stick together through the day, trading conspiracy theories and complaints about our crappy environment. It makes the long hours more bearable, and it gives me hope. At least *somebody* besides Sophia and I are trying to figure Omega out. Most of the prisoners here are zoned out. Desperate and terrified.

I might have plenty of fear to go around, but I haven't given up yet. Omega might be scary, but they're also infuriating. They make me angry. This is our *home*, and they have no right being here, treating us like dirt.

I want them taken down. Hard.

And the first step towards taking down an enemy is familiarization. Know what you're up against. That's what Chris would tell me. Learn everything you can about your opponent, their strengths and weaknesses, and then attack. Not that I'm planning on taking down the entire Omega army, of course, but it gives me a sense of security to know that Omega is *very* human and very *real*. If they can be figured out, then they can be destroyed.

And that wouldn't hurt my feelings.

Not one bit.

Chapter Five

Omega should go ahead and give classes in world domination, because they've got the formula down to a science. I don't know how far their invasion extends - or whether or not the United States is the only one affected by it - but I do know this: they're smart. Organized. Utilizing resources that are already here, enslaving the population that was already in place. Things are working out fine and dandy for them, while the civilian population is being forced to march through cold showers and do manual labor.

Yeah.

I'd say people like me could have been better prepared for a situation like this. It's odd, too. I was probably the only person in Los Angeles with an emergency go-bag, a getaway car and a pre-planned emergency rendezvous point when the EMP hit. I was ready and prepared. Naïve? Yes. Scared? You bet. But I was actually *ready*. Apparently someone needs to write a survival manual about labor camps, because now I'm *not* prepared. I'm at Omega's mercy, and that seriously ticks me off.

I hate being bossed around.

Enslavement isn't my fantasy job.

But there are things I can do to keep myself alive and well while many of the other prisoners shrivel up and waste away. For one thing, mental stimulation is a big part of keeping myself sharp. I play games with myself. I solve riddles. I recite memory verses. Whatever I can do to keep my mind working.

Sophia and I tell each other stories, everything from the *Three Little Pigs* to *Goodnight Moon* to avoid going crazy. Or maybe the fact that we're reciting *Goodnight Moon* out loud is a sign of our insanity. Whatever. It helps the time pass quicker.

The food that we receive isn't enough to keep me healthy and strong, either, so Sophia and I have started eating some of the oranges we pick. It's a potentially lethal situation, because if we get caught eating the food that we're supposed to be picking, we could very well be killed. Just like that. And I have a feeling Kamaneva would dance a Russian jig over my grave.

The oranges are full of Vitamin C, though, which keeps us healthier than the rest of the prisoners. But I'm sure we're not the only ones bending the rules. I mean, if you *don't* fly under the radar, you'll die. You'll burn out and turn into a hollow shell of yourself. I've seen it happen.

An older woman named Jenna arrived at the labor camp a few days ago, and she's already lost. She's retreated far inside of herself, refusing to speak, refusing to eat. She worked until she dropped unconscious in the fields. The guards kicked her awake. Forced to begin working again.

She's given up hope. She's already dead.

I don't want to turn into that.

I want to *live*.

I want to see Chris again. And Dad. And the Youngs.

It's not like it's the ultimate dream to live at a death camp. More like the ultimate nightmare. Because a labor camp will eventually get you to one place: an early grave. Chris would agree with that. He'd tell me to figure a way out of this mess.

Well, I'm *trying.*

There's not a lot I can do with Kamaneva and her hyperactive guards stalking our every move. It's not like I can smuggle in the back of a pickup truck and sneak out the front gate, either. Omega checks and double-checks every vehicle that goes in and out of the camp.

I'm stuck.

Stuck, stuck, stuck.

"We're not *stuck,*" Sophia corrects. "We're *enslaved*. There's a difference."

"Care to elaborate, oh philosophical one?"

"Stuck implies that we can't move because we just *can't* or *won't.* We're actually being *temporarily detained* by evil people."

"Like I said. We're stuck." My fingers close around an orange, and judging by the amount of growling my stomach is doing, I could really use a bite. "You know what I would give for a big greasy taco right now?"

"What would you give?" she sighs.

"I have no idea. Anything, probably."

"Me too."

Well, not *anything*. I wouldn't be willing to lose my life over it. Then again, there's no telling what I might be willing to go through for a taco. Enter my current climate of reasoning, a testament to the fact that I may be taking a ride on the crazy train a lot sooner than I think if I don't get out of this place.

"Hey," Harry whispers, approaching us. His bag is slung over his shoulder. "Want to know what I just heard?"

"Let me guess," I say. "Kamaneva's going to let us have pudding cups with our meals. Oh, joy."

"No." He frowns, looking puzzled. Harry doesn't get my humor. "I overheard some of the guards discussing the backup generators."

"What about them?"

"They're going to start using them for cold storage."

"Why?" Sophia asks.

"So they can store all of this food we're harvesting for them," I say. "They've *got* to be saving this for somebody, because they're not shipping all of it out anymore."

"Who do you think is coming?" Harry asks.

"I told you before. Backup."

"But *where* is their backup coming from?" Sophia presses.

I wipe the sweat off my forehead, thinking.

"We're on the West Coast, right?"

"Duh."

"It was a rhetorical question." I roll my eyes. "What country is closest to us?"

Harry shrugs.

"Oh, come on," I say. China, anyone?"

"You don't know that China is sending backup troops for Omega. We don't even know who Omega *is* anyway," Sophia replies. "If we don't know who Omega is, then there's no way we can know who's helping them."

"I've got a pretty good idea," I reply, raising an eyebrow. "All you have to do is think about all the countries that might have a motive to attack the United States. That's, like, the entire universe."

"So you're saying the whole world is against us?"

"No. I'm saying I think we can be pretty sure that Russia is involved, and maybe North Korea. North Korea doesn't have enough troops or the technology to invade the United States on their own. China does. China's entire population is an army."

"Then which one of those countries sent out the EMP? And who's nuking the East Coast – if that's even true?" Sophia asks.

"Does it really matter?" I say. "If they're all working together, then it was a joint effort. Hooray for teamwork, I guess."

"Where's the rest of the world?" Sophia sighs. "What happened to them? Are we the only country affected by this?"

"That's a good question," I admit. "I would think one of our allies would come help us out...but not even our own military can help us, so maybe that's a stupid question." I stop and look up at Harry, who's watching me with a curious expression. "What?"

"Nothing." A small smile appears on his face. "You're just very good at figuring things out, that's all."

"Do I get an A for effort?"

"Sure."

"Do you ever think about escaping?" Sophia whispers suddenly.

Harry and I stiffen at the mention of the "e-word." That's a trigger word. Instant death. I lower my voice. "Of course. I wouldn't be human if I didn't."

"It can't be done, can it?" she stares off through the trees, her gaze stopping at the barbed wire fencing. "We really are...*stuck*."

"Nah." I nudge her shoulder. "I'm willing to give it the old college try at some point, aren't you?"

"I don't want to end up dead."

"She's got a valid point," Harry says.

"We'll end up dead either way," I point out. "Either we'll be worked to death or we'll die escaping. One of these days..." I trail off, knowing it's wiser to keep my mouth shut. Just because the idea of escaping is an attractive thought doesn't mean I should go blabbing about it. You never know who you can trust, especially in a place like this. It's like high school on steroids. Backstabbers, cliques, and nasty teachers all thrown into the same crummy mix. Only the penalty for messing up is a lot worse than suspension.

It's sudden death.

Fun times, right?

At the end of the day when our work is finally done, the guards round us up and march us back into the school compound. But instead of heading towards the cafeteria like we *always* do, we stop in what used to be the outdoor cafeteria. Now it's just a patch of dead grass. A wilted, hand painted banner is falling off the far wall. It says, *Walk for a Cure*. I swallow. Reminders of normalcy are everywhere.

And then there's *this.*

Kamaneva is waiting patiently in the center of the courtyard, watching the prisoners file in.

"One of you has been stealing from me," she states.

The lump in my throat turns into a baseball. I can feel Sophia tensing up beside me, so I put a hand on her wrist. I stare straight ahead, motionless. Afraid to give myself away with just the slightest twitch of a facial muscle.

"I don't know which one of you it is," she goes on, taking a few calculating steps, "but when I *do* find out, do you know what the punishment is for stealing from me?"

Nobody answers. We all know. Execution.

The end.

If I were wearing boots, I'd be shaking in them. Instead all I can do is stand and tremble in my cheap sandals, avoiding eye contact. Eating oranges have been keeping Sophia and I a little healthier and stronger than the rest of the women in our group, and if Kamaneva ever notices that, she just might catch on. But right now, the two of us look disheveled and unhealthy despite our efforts. That happens when you haven't had a bath in weeks and you're wearing thrift store reject clothes covered in dirt and filth.

Kamaneva studies the group. Her eyes eventually fall on me – like always. I stare at the wall. I will myself to remain emotionless. Just one wrong move and I'm toast. After a nerve-racking five seconds, she moves her gaze to the next person in line. I release a small breath. Sophia squeezes my hand.

By the time we make it into the cafeteria, my knees are almost knocking together because I'm trembling so badly. I sit down with Sophia at our spot in the corner. Harry approaches us. "What was that all about?" he wonders. "Was that really necessary on Kamaneva's part?"

"She's just trying to scare us," I say.

Harry doesn't know that Sophia and I have been eating oranges. The less people who know, the better. The more people who know your secrets, the higher the potential for them to betray you.

"Well, I'm effectively scared," Harry replies.

"Who knows if somebody's really even stealing from her?" I say. "She could have made up the whole story just to put everybody on edge. To keep us all on our best behavior."

Harry shrugs.

"It's possible, I suppose."

Yeah. It's possible. Only I know the truth.

I concentrate on eating my food. It feels as if everyone is watching me, waiting for me to give myself away. It's miserable. It's the prison camp environment. Nobody trusts anybody else, and we're all afraid of being stabbed in the back.

Maybe I was right.

Maybe this is a lot more like high school than I thought.

Chapter Six

Four weeks in a labor camp is enough to make anyone grouchy. My clothes are worn through with holes and my body is coated with a thick layer of dirt. I'm slowly starving, dehydrated, lonely, scared and desperate to escape. The only problem is, there isn't any easy way out of this camp.

Thirty days of observation has only told me two things that *might* be considered a weakness:

1. Even with all of the trucks and plumbing Omega has inside the school complex, the portable generators that they've installed isn't enough to keep all the lights in the camp running. The back stretch of the fence is dark, but as far as I can tell, heavily patrolled.
2. Grease, the Omega soldier with the bad hair, seems to have gained sympathy for Sophia and I. He might come in handy.
3. I've pretty much got the routine of the guards figured out, and I know which troopers are lazier or less intelligent than the rest.

Omega is armed, powerful and dangerous. I, on the other hand, am tired, tiny and afraid. There's nothing I can do. Omega never slips up. They don't leave weapons lying around for me to steal. They don't leave stretches of the fence unguarded. They're on top of everything, and Kamaneva is on top of everybody in Group 13. The woman has gotten considerably crueler in the last couple of weeks. She's begun daily torture treatments and public punishments to keep the workforce under control. Every once in a while one of the officers will round up the prisoners, grab a worker for a real or imagined violation of a regulation, and beat or execute them on the spot.

It keeps everybody in line.

Omega has moved us from orange fields to empty fields. They're making us prepare for planting, although I'm not sure what we're going to plant yet. I'm guessing it will be something high in nutritional value. Something to keep an army going. And judging by the amount of prisoners being brought in and forced to work, I'm guessing Omega is planning on hosting a whole lot of troops. Soon.

That's not a rosy prospect.

Everyone has a different idea about who Omega is, why they're here, and what they want. In my opinion, it's really not that much of a mystery anymore. Omega is a cover name to keep us confused. Global forces are involved. There's no other explanation. They need slave labor to keep the invading troops fed, and who better than to provide that kind of work than people like me?

But what is their final goal? What's the point of this invasion?

Power, wealth or greed, probably. The usual suspects. Besides. Who wouldn't want to take down the United States, right?

"If you ever get the chance to escape," I tell Sophia and Harry over dinner one night, "take it. Don't wait for anybody else. Don't think. Just go. Take the opportunity."

"I couldn't leave without you," Sophia says firmly.

I close my eyes, because I don't believe that. In the end, it all comes down to self-preservation. If Sophia saw an opening to escape, she'd take it without looking back. So would Harry.

And so would I.

Wouldn't I? Wouldn't *Chris*?

Yes. Chris would escape and then find a way to come back and get me out. He would never throw away an opportunity to stay alive. He's just that kind of person.

"I just..." I begin, but trail off. "I appreciate that."

"You're all I have." Sophia's eyes go glassy with tears. "We're like family now."

"I'm sure your family is alive in New York," I say, touching her shoulder.

"Not if the rumors are true and New York was nuked." Sophia hunches closer to the table, looking at the floor. "Then they're all dead. My parents, my brother...they'd be gone."

"We don't know if that's true."

"I heard *all* the major cities were nuked," Harry adds.

I slap his arm as Sophia pales even more.

"I mean...not all. Just some." He tries to smile. "Honestly, how are we supposed to separate reality from rumors?"

"With common sense," I say.

Easier said than done.

At that moment, Kamaneva walks into the cafeteria. She's wearing her blue uniform, knee-high boots and signature skin-stretching bun. Her eyes scan the room. She slowly walks down the center aisle of the cafeteria. We stop eating. Sudden silence falls over the room.

Kamaneva stops at our table. Sophia keeps her head down. Harry's fingers are trembling around the brim of his soup bowl. I'm the only one who's not afraid to look Kamaneva in the eye. I don't say a word. Not that there isn't a lot of sarcasm dying to get out of me...I just know better than to challenge her that bluntly.

She motions for me to stand up. I do.

"I believe I've found our thief," she states.

And there it is. Just like that. A lead weight drops to the pit of my stomach. A twisted sneer spreads across her face. I can tell she's been waiting for this moment. It's probably the highly of her day.

I glance at Harry and Sophia, but their eyes are glued to the floor. Harry is shaking. They look worse than I do.

"How-" I begin, but Kamaneva cuts me off.

"I have my sources," she says.

Her eyes flick to Harry. He swallows and the food I just ate turns over in my stomach. He won't look at me.

"You...?" I whisper.

He still doesn't say anything.

"Why?" I demand, tears springing to my eyes.

Sophia is shocked. Frozen. Kamaneva wraps her fingers around my arm and pulls me away from the table, pushing me towards two Omega troopers. Sophia suddenly starts screaming.

"You *traitor!*" she shrieks, lunging at Harry.

He crashes to the ground with Sophia on top of him. She claws at his face, pummels his chest with her fists. Kamaneva watches in silence. Guards break up the fight, and when Sophia is hauled to her feet, her face is covered with tears. Harry appears stricken.

Add me to the list.

"She made me tell you," Harry says. "I swear, Cassidy, I wouldn't do anything like this unless-"

"-Unless your life depended on it?" I snort. "I guess it did."

He nods, fisting his hands and sinking to the ground.

Kamaneva and her guards drag me outside. The next thing I know, I'm being led through the school to a storage building behind the complex. And the whole time, all I can think is:

Harry betrayed me.

"What did you do to Harry?" I demand, shaking with rage. "What did you threaten him with?"

Kamaneva doesn't answer.

"You made him do that." I struggle against the guards, total rage turning my vision red. "Why are you doing this to me? Why do you hate me so much? I never did *anything* to you!"

"You're alive," Kamaneva snaps, cold. "My *daughter* should have been alive."

The storage facility is a small building with a tiny window near the ceiling. The guards open the doors and throw me inside. I land on my hands and knees, looking at a blank room. It's empty. Not even a bench or a bucket to use for a toilet.

"You want to kill me and Sophia because your daughter died?" I shake my head. "You're insane."

Kamaneva flushes and lands a heavy kick to my side. I double over and jump to my feet, drawing back. "Only one of you has to die," she hisses. "It's only fair."

"I'm not the one who killed your daughter."

"My daughter died when she was about your age." Kamaneva's features don't soften. They remain steely and emotionless.

"It wasn't my fault," I say.

She looks me up and down. "The prisoners have to be kept in line. You violated the rules. You have until morning."

She spins on her heel. The guards slam and lock the heavy door behind them. The building is plunged into darkness. It's cold. Empty. Lonely. I pace, trying to process everything that just happened.

Harry turned me in for stealing. Kamaneva must have given him something in return. Extra rations? A bed to sleep on? Who the heck knows? She's a borderline sociopath who loves the drama of dragging out an execution. I had no idea the woman hated me that much. Scratch that. Hated *Sophia* and me. What's worse, Chris was right. I really *can't* trust anybody.

Harry betrayed me.

You don't know what Kamaneva did to him to get him to do this, my conscious points out. *She probably threatened to have him killed. He didn't have a choice.*

No. We all have a choice. I never would have betrayed Sophia or Harry.

And Chris *never* would have betrayed me.

I curl up in a ball in the front corner of the building. My mouth is dry, my heart is beating fast. A wave of fresh, raw fear washes over me. Tears blur my vision.

Tomorrow, Kamaneva will come back for me.

Tomorrow, I'll be executed.

Chapter Seven

I've been in life or death situations before. How many times did I almost die when I was trying to find my father after the EMP hit? More times than I'd like to count.

This situation is different, because all you can do is sit and wait for death to come knocking at your door. You can't fight it. You can't do anything about it. You can only hope that you'll survive.

But that's not going to happen. Not now.

Dawn has arrived. Slits of sunlight are falling through the single window near the roof of the storage building. I'm standing with my back pressed against the far wall, studying the words and phrases etched into the wall by prisoners that have been locked in this room before me. Everything from names and dates to Bible verses has been scratched into the paint. Someone wrote:

Rose Leland

Reedley, California

Don't Forget Me

A final note. I fight the tears prickling behind my eyes. Breaking down isn't going to do any good at this point. My fate is sealed. And now that the hysterics have passed and I've accepted this fact, I'm swamped with an eerie calm feeling.

I feel as if I'm stuck in a dream. A bad dream, one in which I know what the outcome will be. One in which I can do nothing to change it.

I rub my thumb along the gold shield necklace Chris gave me so many months ago. If he knew I was about to die, would he tell me he loved me? I don't know. I don't think I *want* to know.

But I can hope.

Thirty minutes after sunrise, I footsteps approach the building. My muscles tense. Sounds become sharper, louder. My fear is a physical thing. I'm going to die. I'm going to be executed.

No one will remember that I existed.

Suddenly frightened at the prospect of being forgotten, I pick up a small shard of metal from the floor. I scratch my name into the dark paint on the wall, leaving CASSIDY HART in white letters. There. At least I've memorialized myself somewhere. It's not like I'm going to get a funeral. They'll probably throw my dead body into a ditch…

The door rattles, breaking me out of my morbid thoughts. Kamaneva steps inside, four Omega guards with her. I tilt my head to look up at her from my crouched position on the floor. She takes in my appearance and smiles – not in a friendly, fuzzy way, either. It's more like a twisted leer of satisfaction.

So not helping.

"Ready?" she asks.

I say nothing. I simply glare.

Two Omega guards pull me upright, and that's when I notice that one of the troopers with Kamaneva is Grease. He's looking at me with sad eyes. I lock gazes with him and he frowns before looking away.

And that's it.

I'm taken out of the storage building and led through the center of the school. We pass the *LAB* and the cafeteria. By the time I'm brought to the front of the school, a crowd of POWs have gathered. A curving section of the road dips close to the front sidewalk, widening near a series of steps that lead to a dry fountain. It used to be a school bus parking area.

Now it's a stage for prisoner executions.

There are hundreds of POWs watching. Kamaneva has turned this into performance – an example of discipline. I'm led to the center of the road, up the steps to the fountain. The Omega troopers release me. Kamaneva takes a step forward and gestures to Grease.

"Kill her," she says. A simple statement.

So simple, so horrible.

He doesn't move, appearing stricken. I don't even *try* to resist. Why would I? I'll be shot if I attempt to escape, and I'll be shot if I don't. I'm a dead girl either way.

"Let this be a lesson to everyone here," Kamaneva growls, her public speaking voice emerging. "Look at Cassidy Hart and witness what happens if you disobey."

I raise my head, suddenly angry,

A rush of satisfaction fills my heart. It's as if the crowd of prisoners isn't even there. There's no stage fright, no humiliation. I'm furious and hey, I'm about to be executed. I might as well say what I want to say.

"You can kill me," I state, lifting my chin, "and you can kill everyone in this camp, one by one. But you can't kill the desire to be free. Somebody will take you down. It *will* happen."

Kamaneva's jaw is tight. Her cheeks redden.

"You're replaceable."

"I've got news for you," I reply. "You're replaceable, too."

The crowd murmurs softly. Kamaneva's eyes dart to Grease.

"Give me your weapon," she commands, referring to the handgun he's holding. "Let's get this over with."

I swallow and fist my hands at my sides.

So this is how it ends for Cassidy Hart? She gets shot in the head by a crazy woman at a bus stop? Not the glamorous death I'd envisioned for myself. I'd always pictured myself dying some kind of tragic death. The type of death where I'm laid in a glass coffin and people wait in a line to look at me and say nice things.

Not that I have an ego or anything.

"Any final words?" Kamaneva asks, taking Grease's weapon.

"Yeah." I make a monumental effort to keep my lower lip from trembling. "I didn't go down without a fight." I turn to the crowd. "And neither should *any of you*!"

Kamaneva lifts the gun, pointblank range, muzzle to my forehead.

This is it. My ears fill with the frantic beating of my heart. My vision turns hazy as I stare down the cold, steely bore of the gun. I blink and tears run down my cheeks. I curl my fingers into fists to control my shaking.

I hear the crack of a gunshot and jerk backwards, expecting a short burst of pain. Light at the end of a tunnel. Blood. Something. But instead I hear screaming. I open my eyes and stare at Kamaneva. She's on the ground, shrieking in pain, clutching her side. Blood is soaking her jacket.

A long burst of automatic fire erupts, and a second later two Omega guards are sprawled dead on the ground. The prisoners *freak*. They run in all directions, panic setting in. I search the trees and the school property line for the source of the gunfire. I see nothing.

Omega guards are shoving and firing.

I leap to my feet and sprint away from Kamaneva, weaving my way into the panicked mob. Omega guards are scrambling to close the gate around the prison, randomly firing into the crowd. In the midst of the chaos, Grease shoves his way through the crowd and grabs my arms.

"Come on!" he yells.

I pull away and plunge into the crowd, squirming out of his reach.

"Cassidy, if you want to live you *have* to stay with me," he continues, chasing after me. I ignore him, fear pumping through my system.

Fear and a lot of *shock*.

I came way too close to getting shot in the head.

"Cassidy, I'm with *Chris*!" Grease shouts.

I spin around, gaping. Did I hear what I thought I heard?

"You have to believe me," he says.

Stunned, I open my mouth to reply, but my words are lost as a massive explosion rocks the school. I'm thrown backwards by the impact. Heat hits my face and the front stretch of the gate outside the administrative building bursts into pieces. Heat and flames lick around the edges. Omega troops as well as prisoners are flat on their backs (or faces), groping, trying to regain their balance. My ears are ringing, making everything just *that* much more confusing.

A wave of men push through the front entrance, guns blazing, systematically working their way onto the property. I struggle to my feet, looking at their clothes. Worn pants and boots, rifles. Blue bands of cloth tied around their upper right arms.

Blue?

I search the crowd for Grease. He's saying something, but between the ringing in my ears and the background noise, I can barely make it out. Something like, *Follow me!*

"You're with Chris *Young*?" I ask.

He nods.

There's no way logic can factor into what I do next. I jump up and follow the man because of two words: *Chris Young.*

As I struggle to keep up with Grease, a trooper on the ground jams his boots into my legs, knocking me off my feet. I hit the ground hard. The air rushes out of my lungs.

I roll to the side, just out of his reach, and crawl towards an Omega man who's unconscious on the ground. As I do, the rapid sound of gunfire peppers the camp as the mystery men with the blue armbands flood the area, picking off...*Omega soldiers.*

They're not hurting *prisoners.*

Realization slowly dawns. Omega is being attacked. By the *good guys.* Whoever the "good guys" are. I don't know and I don't care. I grab an obnoxiously huge gun off the unconscious trooper's body and get to my feet, determined to do something to help.

I have no idea where Grease went. I lost him in the crowd. I look over the weapon, looking for a safety switch. No such luck. I don't recognize this weapon. I squeeze the trigger...barely. A spray of bullets razes the administrative wall next to me, hitting a few Omega troopers in the process. I let go of the trigger and take a few steps backwards, blinking at the downed men.

Oh. That would be *my* handiwork, I guess.

Five Omega men are charging towards the front gate, preparing to take on the advancing enemy – the Blue Bands. I squeeze the trigger again and take the whole group down with one sweep of the gun. I haven't killed them. Their legs have been shot out from under them, sending them sprawling.

I swallow, and a shout of exhilaration bursts out of my mouth as adrenaline surges like fire in my veins.

This is *war,* isn't it?

I squeeze the trigger again in an attempt to scare off more troopers from the front gate. I don't get anything but an empty click. Nothing. I drop the weapon. I don't have any more ammunition. I turn to run, smacking into Grease. He grabs me by the arms.

"Not bad shooting, kid," he says. "For a girl."

"Jerk."

"You need to come with me now."

He keeps a steady grip on my arm.

"Where?" I demand, hesitating. "Where's *Chris*?"

Another explosion detonates on the other side of the schoolyard. The sound of glass shattering and people screaming fills the air. Black, acrid smoke fills the sky, making my eyes tear up.

"I'm taking you to Chris." He pulls me forward. "Look, I'm not the enemy here. I just killed Kamaneva."

"Whoa. *You*?"

And that's the extent of our five-second conversation. Because all hell has broken loose in the school. Windows are being blown out, bullets are flying everywhere. Prisoners are sprinting away from the building and Omega troopers are rushing around the perimeter, attempting to close the civilians in and keep the Blue Bands out.

It's not working very well.

"We're in trouble," Grease says.

I follow his line of sight. A few Omega troops are pointing at Grease, and next thing I know, we're being fired at. I duck for cover behind the edge of the front administrative building, barely missing a bullet to the head.

"Why are they shooting at *you*?"

"Because I just committed treason." He stands up and smashes the office window apart with the butt of his gun. "Come on. We have to take cover."

Right. My dad told me once, back when he was still an active-duty cop in LA, that concealment and cover are two different things. Concealment is when you're hidden from your enemies, but if they see you for some reason, they can still shoot you. Cover is anything that will physically stop a bullet. Your enemy might know you're there, but they can't hurt you.

I prefer cover to concealment.

Grease swings his legs over the windowsill. I follow, crawling along the floor of an office. Probably the principal's. But all of the personal belongings and photos have been removed, replaced with cold, sterile ornaments. A Russian flag is sticking out of a pencil cup. A black Omega flag is on the wall. That's about as cute and comfortable as this place gets.

We stay low as we push through the office, flinging open a door to the hallway. Grease doesn't enter right away. He checks the hall and then waves me forward. The Omega troopers reach the window and open fire inside the office. I lunge into the hall, barely missing being shot…for the fiftieth time today.

It's getting to be a bad habit.

We move down the hall. Smoke is seeping out of most of the rooms, making it difficult to navigate and breathe at the same time. Thankfully, Grease seems to have a good idea of where he's going. As we round a corner, he suddenly drops to his knees and jerks me down with him. Omega troopers are coming up on us from the front and behind. We're trapped. I crouch next to him, heart pounding, waiting for him to come up with a brilliant plan.

"Do something!" I say.

He moves backwards and disappears into an office with an open door. It's filled with black, choking smoke. I dive in after him, staying low to the ground. Trying to breathe. Flames are crawling up the walls, slapping my cheeks with raw heat.

"This wasn't what I had in mind," I mutter.

"Here," Grease calls, slipping through a door on the right. It leads to another office. We run inside just in time to come nose to nose with three Omega men making their way down the center of the building.

Surrounded on three sides by troopers in a burning building?

We're so dead.

"Stay down," Grease warns, shouldering his weapon.

I stay covered behind the wall of the burning office. Omega troopers are going to come up behind us in a few seconds, and then I'll have no place to hide. Grease fires a few bursts from his rifle. Two troopers drop to the ground. But there are plenty more where they came from. They unleash a flurry of fire. Furniture splinters. Glass shatters.

Things aren't looking so good, but Grease doesn't seem as wired as me. He seems focused. "Duck," he says.

I cover my head with my hands. He turns his body slightly to shield mine. Something detonates at the far end of the building, sending pieces of wood and plaster everywhere. My ears start ringing *again*. Blue Bands jump inside the building through windows on the far side, working their way through the cubicles like a SWAT team on a raid.

They've got scarves tied around their mouths, sunglasses shielding their eyes from the smoke. I stay next to Grease, wondering if I should stay put or run for my life. Because even though these people are beating up Omega, they could still have the potential to hurt *me*.

The Blue Band in the lead blasts killing gunfire into the troopers coming up through the front – the guards that originally chased Grease and I inside. He does it quickly and smoothly, without hesitation. His team fans out around him, checking the dead and dying. Grease stands up, holding his gun above his head with both hands. I expect him to be shot on sight since he's wearing an Omega uniform – but they seem to recognize him.

The Blue Band in the lead approaches him, weapon ready, then lowers it and slaps Grease on the back.

"Nice work," he says.

I scramble to my feet, recognizing that voice instantly.

Grease steps aside and the Blue Band pulls his scarf down around his mouth, taking off the sunglasses. Green eyes, dark hair pulled back in a ponytail. The most beautiful sight I've ever seen.

"Chris!" I run forward and tackle him, wrapping my arms around his neck. I breathe in his familiar scent – only today he smells a little sweatier than usual. I blame it on warfare.

"Cassie," he says, holding me at arm's length. He looks me over from head to toe. "Are you hurt?"

"That's kind of a loaded question." I'm grinning from ear to ear, actually. "I can't believe you're here! I can't even-"

He steps forward and crushes me against his chest with one arm, pulling me into a fierce kiss. My heart stops beating. His fingers dig into my waist and, for a short moment, there's no one here but the two of us.

And then it's back to reality.

"Yo, boss. Heads up!" Grease yells.

Chris breaks the kiss, leaving me flushed with color as he picks me up with one arm and moves me out of the way. I grab his arm as he calmly shoots an Omega trooper who'd been creeping towards us in the hallway.

Sneaky.

"How did you know where to find me?" I ask, breathless.

Chris pulls me backwards with his team – whoever they are – and pulls his scarf back over his mouth. "Long story," he says, nodding at Grease, who's ditched the Omega jacket and tied a blue armband around his upper arm. "I'll explain later. Right now just do what I say and don't ask questions, okay?"

I nod, disappointed.

Our happy reunion didn't last long, did it?

I'm still dazed when we exit through a broken window and enter an empty playground area. Hopscotch squares are painted on the ground. Playground equipment has been left untouched.

We stay close to the side of the building, since it gives us more cover than if we were running down the middle of the sidewalk. We've got five people with us – four Blue Bands and Grease. Something's off.

"Who are all these people?" I ask. "Soldiers?"

"Local militia," Chris answers. "We've been...hold it." He pauses. "Max?"

Grease nods. He checks the corner and gives us the all clear. We run forward, entering the bus stop area where I was almost killed a mere few minutes ago. The front gate around the school has been totaled. A couple dozen Blue Bands are ravaging what's left of the facility, setting it on fire, shooting it up, blowing it up. Whatever they can do to be a pain.

Omega is in total disarray. I search for Kamaneva on the ground, but her body isn't there. She could still be alive, then. Great. "Let's shut this party down," Chris says, rounding up the Blue Bands. He whistles loudly and makes a circular motion over his head. "Let's move out," he yells. "Rally point Echo!" The militiamen have commandeered pickup trucks from the fields and thrown the ladders and buckets out. They're loading half of them up with fuel containers and boxes of food and supplies. The other trucks are being stuffed with liberated prisoners.

"Cassidy!"

I turn at the sound of Sophia's voice. She runs towards me, grabbing me in a frantic embrace. It's kind of painful. "Oh, my God, I thought Kamaneva killed you," she says, crying. "I'm so glad you're okay."

"Me too." I glance at Chris. He's calm. "I think we were just liberated by a small army."

"Who?"

"Don't know. Chris is with them, though."

"Your boyfriend?"

I make an *I guess so* gesture.

Sophia stares at him. "Wow."

The few Omega troopers that aren't retreating into the orchards or haven't been killed yet try to pull off a last ditch effort to keep the prisoners from escaping by rushing the pickup trucks like kamikaze warriors. The Blue Bands are ready for them, though. Gunfire rips through the air as Chris grabs me by the waist, shoulders me into the front seat of a pickup truck, and sets me down in the middle seat. Sophia jumps onto the rear bed with a bunch of other prisoners who are both standing and sitting. Grease swings himself into the driver's seat and slams the door shut. The windows have been rolled down. Chris is sitting shotgun, his weapon ready.

And here I am in the middle of it.

Life is so weird.

"Go," Chris commands.

Grease floors it. The pickup surges forward. I'm thrown against the seat. The only thing that doesn't send me flying out the open window is my death grip on Chris's left arm. The other pickups are following our lead. We roar over what used to be the security fence. Remains of barbed wire and metal are lying twisted on the ground. I turn around in my seat and stare at the school. It's a barbecue. Totaled. The buildings are destroyed, the grounds are burning and there are dead Omega troopers everywhere. Unbelievable.

I face Chris.

"Who are these people?" I whisper, trembling.

"Friends," he replies, kissing my forehead.

"*Your* friends?"

"*Our* friends."

"Well, that's a first. I have *friends* now."

He turns to focus on the road, giving directions to Grease and watching for enemies. But I don't think Omega will be able to get backup troops in fast enough to stop us.

Shocked and bewildered, I focus on what's in front of us. Country roads, orchards, abandoned farmhouses and, in the distance, the foothills. Beyond that are the mountains.

"Where are we going?" I ask.

"Away from here," Grease replies. "And by the way, you can call me Max."

I watch Sophia hanging on for dear life in the rearview mirror, wondering how many other trucks we've got following us in this freedom convoy. Probably five or six. A final, giant explosion lights up the early morning sky above the school. It's the biggest detonation I've ever seen. A pillar of flames rolls through the air, turning inside out with inky black smoke. It mushrooms in all directions.

The school is gone.

"Mission accomplished," Chris remarks.

"You've got a lot of explaining to do," I say, cocking an eyebrow.

"Yeah?" Chris leans closer. "I'm not the only one."

He has a point. This could be a long road trip.

Chapter Eight

We drive for several hours. We haven't been ambushed or blown up, so I take that as a positive sign. Negatively, I'm suffering from the aftershock of nearly being publically executed by a Russian psychopath. Despite the warmth of the cab, I'm shivering from head to toe.

A classic symptom of shock.

Chris senses my discomfort.

"Cassie? Are you okay?"

"Yeah, I'm just...a little wiped out, I guess."

I'm a lousy liar. He frowns and tips my chin up with his finger, looking at my eyes. "Are you sick? Wounded? Be honest with me."

"Neither." I lean against his shoulder. "I almost got shot in the head. Give me a couple seconds to recover."

Grease – *Max* – stifles a laugh.

"What's so funny?" I demand. "You know, I don't get you. One second you're an Omega soldier, and then you're all chummy with rogue militiamen from God-knows-where. *And* you shot Kamaneva. What made you turn on Omega?"

Chris chuckles, sliding his arm around my shoulders, drawing me close to his chest. "Max was never *for* Omega in the first place, Cassie," he says. "He's always been a spy for us."

"Who's *us*?"

"This militia," Max says. "We're called the Free Army. But...we're not really big enough to be considered an army."

"That's not entirely true," Chris points out. "We *did* just level an entire labor camp with a couple dozen men. Not a bad day's work."

"Okay, since when have you been involved with a rebel army?" I ask Chris, looking up at him. "Last I saw you, you were going hunting. And you were *late.*"

He brushes my bangs out of my eyes.

"Yeah, I was." He moves closer, feeling the rough ends of my hair between his fingers. "I'm sorry, Cassie. When I came back and you were gone, I looked everywhere for you. It didn't take me long to figure out what happened."

"We ran into each other a couple of weeks after you got picked up by Omega," Max adds. "They had just raided a community in the hills and taken most of the people there as prisoners."

Sophia's community.

"Max was a narcotics officer back in Sacramento," Chris explains. "He was an undercover agent."

"A real secret agent?" I ask, awed.

"Kind of. I'd go undercover and pose as a drug dealer. Work a case. Get the bad guys." He shrugs. "Like what I just did with Omega."

"It's dangerous work," Chris concludes. "Max is a perfect spy."

"But Max was *there* during my first day at the prison camp."

"Yeah, I've been spying on Omega for a few months now," Max replies.

"Here's what happened," Chris explains, smiling at my confused expression. "I found the Free Army not long after they took you to the labor camp. There were only a few men at that point. Not a lot of organization. Not really any leadership. A good bunch of men, though."

"How did you find out where I was?" I ask.

"Max." Chris takes a deep breath. "He was already a spy. He'd been delivering messages to the militia anyway, and I contacted him to see if you were at the labor camp. Obviously you were, so I started planning."

"How did you get all these people to help you?"

"This labor camp is a pretty big link in Omega's supply chain," Chris says. "They're using prisoners to send food to other troops, plus they've got fuel supplies and backup generators. Taking this out hurt them, plus I got you back."

"So this was an attack...not just a rescue mission?"

"Correct. A lot of these prisoners will join the militia. We need new soldiers, anyway." Chris nudges my forehead with the tip of his nose. "You look puzzled."

"I am!" I sigh. "So now you're in charge of all these people?"

"People tend to follow Chris," Max comments. "It just happened."

"So you *are* in charge."

He shrugs.

Ah. Great. My boyfriend is now in charge of a rebel army leading raids on Omega supply chains. I'm not sure if I should be happy or conflicted about this.

"You look worried," Chris remarks.

"I'm not. I'm just *tired*."

"I know. We'll be there soon."

"Where are we going?"

"Back to base."

I raise an eyebrow.

"I'll explain everything in more detail later," he says in a softer voice, "when you're feeling better."

He's right. I'm too spaced out right now to absorb any more important information. We make our way into the lower foothills, zipping through familiar territory as we pass Squaw Valley. I swallow nervously. Last time I was here, I woke up in the back of a semi-truck with my head crammed into the wall. Won't Omega know that this is the first place to look for escaped prisoners? The same place they picked them up? Won't they figure out that everyone would head back to their homes after they escaped from prison?

"I know what you're thinking," Chris says, ghosting a smile. "And don't worry about it. We'll be safe here."

"Can you read my thoughts?"

"Pretty much."

Just when I feel myself falling asleep, the truck sputters to a halt. I sit up straight, peering at our surroundings. We're high enough in the hills to be considered "in the mountains," but I know better. We're probably around the snowline, putting us at three thousand feet. There are trees, creeks and forests. It smells like pine and wet earth.

"This is it?" I ask.

"This is it." Chris opens the car door and steps outside, holding his hand out for me. "You're going to love this."

I take it. My skin prickles with goosebumps in the cool afternoon air. The rest of the trucks are pulling up behind us. I was right. There's about five or six of them, half of them packed with prisoners. The other half are packed with supplies raided from the camp. Militiamen jump out of the vehicles, surrounding Chris. I stand beside him, uncomfortable with being at the center of the ring.

"Good job, boys," Chris says. "That was some of the best work I've seen from you yet. Omega will be scrambling to figure out what happened. By the time they call in backup, the camp will be gone, and their supplies will be destroyed or ruined."

Cheers all around.

The rest of the militiamen remove their facial scarves and sunglasses, and for the first time I get a glimpse of their faces. Young men and women. Some of them don't even look old enough to be out of high school. But here they are, fighting a war.

And then I see Harry Lydell.

He tries to duck his head and turn to the side to avoid my gaze, but it's too late. The damage is done. I cover my mouth with my hands just as Sophia comes up behind me, pointing.

"What are *you* doing here?" she demands, seething.

"Who is that?" Chris asks, following my line of sight.

"Harry," I say, staring at the ground.

He spreads his arms out, waiting for an explanation.

"You were working with Kamaneva, last time I checked," Max says, walking up to Harry. He grabs him around the collar. Drags him to the center of the trucks. Holds him there. Harry is sweating and shaking.

"Please," he begs, "Kamaneva forced me to turn you in, Cassidy."

"*He* turned you in?" Chris looks surprised. "If you turned her in to Omega, *why* did you think you'd be safe coming with us?"

Chris curls his fingers around the front of Harry's shirt, overshadowing the Englishman's lean frame. His eyes are steely – he's *mad*. "You're a dead man."

"You don't understand," Harry says, choking. "Kamaneva was going to kill me."

Chris gives him a lethal look. The kind of look he usually gives Omega troopers before he beats the crap out of them.

"Kill the traitor," someone hisses.

More people take up the same chant. Every muscle in Chris's body is tense and coiled. His grip on Harry's neck is tight. Lethal.

"Chris," I say, panic rising in my chest. "Stop. He didn't have a choice."

"There's always a choice," Chris grits. "I would have died before I put you in harm's way."

"Yes, because you're strong," I reply. "Harry's not. Let him go."

"This is *not* a game," Chris replies. "He almost got you *killed*."

"Hang him." A random suggestion.

God, are these people insane?

A chorus of agreement echoes throughout the camp. Chris adjusts his vice-like hold on Harry's neck, pulling him in closer. For a moment, I think he's going to say something, but instead he lands a crushing punch to Harry's stomach. The air goes out of him and he doubles over.

"Stop this!" I say, running to Chris. I grab his arm. "You can't kill him."

"If he betrayed you once, he'll betray you twice," Chris replies. His eyes are bright with fury as he draws his handgun. "Get out of the way."

"Just get on with it!" the militiamen urge.

I shove Chris's gun aside. He turns his angry gaze on me and drops Harry, taking a step back. Harry coughs and hacks on his hands and knees. I stand between him and Chris, raising my chin.

"We *can't* execute people," I say. "We'll be no better than Omega if we do."

"Sometimes executions are necessary," Chris spits.

"This piece of filth doesn't deserve to live," Max adds, folding his arms across his chest. "You *do* realize you almost got shot in the head because of him, right?"

"I know *exactly* what he did," I reply, waving my fist in Max's face. "And it's not like I'm ready to give him a free pass out of jail and bake him a cake. I'm saying we *can't* kill him. *Omega* kills people. We can't. We *have* to live by the law of the land – nobody else will if we don't. We're all that's left."

I glare at Chris. A muscle ticks in his jaw. We endure an epic stare-down before he finally turns to Harry. He kicks him *hard* and hauls him up by his shoulders, forcing him to look at me. "Look at her," he growls. "She just saved your worthless life. It won't happen twice."

He shoves him towards Max.

"Give him a job," he commands, taking my arm.

I release a breath, thanking God that this little scene didn't play out the way I thought it might.

We just came *this close* to dissolving into total anarchy.

The tension is palpable as the militiamen disperse. Harry is dragged off by Max. As we leave the trucks behind, I realize that we've parked right outside of a large campsite. Blankets and tents are arranged throughout the wooded areas. Pots and pans, bags of supplies, weaponry. Men wearing the same dark blue armbands are standing guard around the perimeter of the camp. They nod respectfully at Chris as he passes.

"So this is your army?" I whisper.

"You might say that," Chris replies.

"Can I have an army, too? Because that would be awesome."

Chris stops and pulls me aside, pressing me flat against a pine tree.

"Consider it done," he says, kissing me on the lips. I thread my fingers through his long hair, feeling the roughness of his beard scratch my cheeks. "I missed you."

He pulls away to look me in the eyes.

"Not as much as I missed you," I say.

"Doubtful." He strokes my cheek with his thumb. "Do you have any idea what it was like for me when I came back to the trailer and you were gone?"

"I have a general idea." I smile softly. "I'm sorry. There was an Omega trooper inside the house. I don't know how he got in."

"Omega patrol." Chris kisses my forehead. "We need to have a long talk about everything that's happened."

"I agree."

"But first there's something you need to see."

"Does it involve dinner? Or a bath?"

Chris grins.

"Yes, actually."

I take his hand and follow him through the camp. Men and women alike are mingling together, doing chores, stitching up wounds. Some of the females are standing guard along with the men. There's a large makeshift tent set up at the edge of camp, open in the front and closed in the back. Camping chairs and tables are arranged around it. Chris places his hands on my shoulders and pushes me forward.

"Look who's home," he announces.

I give him a puzzled look before a familiar head of blonde hair appears at the mouth of the tent. My jaw drops.

"Isabel?"

Chapter Nine

"Cassidy!"

Twelve-year-old Isabel crosses the space between us and throws her arms around my neck. I hug her back, shocked.

"How...?" I ask.

She pulls back. I smooth her hair away from her face. It's longer than it used to be, but still untamable. Her blue eyes are wide with delight. She's wearing loose cargo pants and boots, her jacket buttoned up to her neck.

"I *can't believe* you're here!" she squeals. "I missed you so much!"

I look to Chris for an explanation. He laughs aloud.

Someone else walks out of the tent.

Chris's mother!

She's wearing old jeans and a plaid button up – just like she was the last time I saw her. Her gray hair is swept into a loose bun.

"Cassidy Hart," she exclaims, pulling me into a warm embrace. "Thank God you're okay."

"How are you here?" I ask. "Seriously. I'm confused here."

"Well, you're about to get a whole lot more confused," a voice says behind me.

Chris's younger brother, Jeff, ambles out of the tent, yanking me into a bear hug. He musses my hair. "What happened to you? What's with that *haircut*?"

I make a face.

"You're one to talk."

His hair is shaggier than I've ever seen it before.

And then Mr. Young steps outside. His appearance is unchanged, but his eyes are sad.

"Cassidy," he says. "Good to see you alive."

I turn in a circle.

"This is *real*, right?" I ask. "Chris? Explain please."

"Why don't you come inside and rest?" Mrs. Young suggests. "We'll explain everything."

Chris slips his arms around my shoulders and leads me inside the tent. I take a seat on a foam mattress, crossing my legs. Isabel snuggles up against my shoulder, wrapping her hands around my arm. "You look weird with short hair," she says.

Oh, the honesty of children.

Jeff settles down beside us. Mrs. Young rummages through a cardboard box of supplies. "You must be starving," she says. "I'll get something for you to eat."

"Don't forget your hungry son, either," Chris comments.

"I won't." She smiles fondly at him. "I was worried about you today."

"I'm back in one piece."

She presses her lips together.

"How are you guys here?" I ask. "Chris and I saw your house burned down. There was *nothing* left. I thought Omega took you!"

"Do you remember when you left to go find your father up at your family cabin a few months ago?" Mrs. Young says, pulling canned goods out of the box. "Chris left the next day to find you. He was so worried."

"I remember," I reply.

"You were gone for a couple of weeks," she continues. "I knew you'd be coming back – Chris wouldn't leave you out there alone. But Omega came."

"I was out hunting," Jeff explains. "I saw them coming. They were burning houses on their way up the hill. I came home and told the folks, and we took off."

"Omega burned the farm and killed the animals," Chris adds.

"Where did you go?" I ask Jeff.

"Here. Well, not here specifically, but to this group." He leans forward. "The Free Army is basically what's left of Squaw Valley. Anybody who hasn't been enslaved, subjugated or killed is right here in this camp."

"They took us in," Mrs. Young adds. "We've been here ever since."

"I found them after you were taken, Cassie," Chris says. "I ran into some of the militia and they took me back to camp. After I found my folks, I started working on finding *you*."

"Mission accomplished," I smile.

"Right." He kisses my fingers. "My family was here the whole time."

"Duh," Isabel mutters. "I can't believe you didn't find us sooner."

"Finding the militia is no simple matter," Mr. Young says. "They're well hidden and you can only find them if they *want* to be found."

"Well, they're much better organized now that Chris is in charge," Mrs. Young sighs, pride lighting her features. "He really changed things around here."

"So what does that make you?" I ask Chris. "Captain? Commander? Boss?"

"I'm not officially in charge of anything," Chris replies, stretching his long legs across the floor. "It just happened."

"People naturally follow Chris," Mrs. Young says.

Max said almost that exact thing during the ride up here.

"Who was in charge before you got here?" I inquire.

"Alexander," Jeff answers, frowning. "But that's another long story. Let's eat."

Mrs. Young removes a portable camping stove from another box.

"Where did you get these supplies?" I ask.

"It's ours," Jeff says. "We loaded up the Hummer you two stole from Omega in December and filled it with our camping supplies before we left the farm. It was a smart move."

"No kidding." I pause. "What do you do about fuel?"

"We steal it." Isabel sits up, grinning. "That's kind of what we do here."

"Steal fuel?"

"No. We raid Omega supplies," Jeff corrects. "We take back food, water, ammunition, weapons and fuel. It hurts them and helps us."

"Destroying that labor camp today will screw up much of their supply line of food in the Central Valley for a while," Chris says. "Plus, other militias will hear about it. It's good for people to know that somebody's fighting back."

"So these people were fighters even *before* you showed up," I say.

"Right." Chris shifts his position, examining his dirt-stained hands.

"Dinner will only take a few minutes," Mrs. Young assures us.

I lean against Chris's shoulder, closing my eyes. For the first time in weeks, I'm not marching to the beat of Omega's drum. There's no roll call, no ten-minute dinner limit, no executions and no Kamaneva.

"You think Kamaneva is still alive?" I ask.

"It's a possibility," Chris says. "But it doesn't matter. The labor camp is totaled."

"That's so unfair," Jeff sighs.

"Don't start that again," Mrs. Young sighs.

"Don't start *what*?" I ask.

"Jeff wants to fight, too," Mrs. Young says. "But he's not ready for combat yet."

"Oh, yeah. I get to stay in camp and guard all the old ladies." Jeff rolls his eyes. "Thrilling." He perks up. Hey, do you still have that knife I gave you?"

My heart sinks.

"No. I haven't seen my backpack since..." I trail off, watching as Chris pulls a knife out of a sheath strapped to his leg. "Is that *mine*?"

"Saved it for you," Chris says.

I take the weapon and turn it over. Yep.

My name is engraved on the handle.

"You're the best," I reply, kissing his cheek.

"I can't argue with that," Chris shrugs.

I look at the knife for a while, remembering when Jeff gave it to me last Christmas. We were all together, then. But one thing was still the same:

My father wasn't there.

"Cassie?" Chris touches my face. "What is it?"

I shake my head.

"Nothing. Just..." I exhale. "I guess nobody's heard any news about my dad?"

Mrs. Young hesitates before answering, dumping a can of beans into a cooking pot. She sets the pot on the stove and gets to work on the rest of the meal.

"No," she says. "I'm sorry, honey. I really am. But your father's situation is a lot different than ours. Omega actually *arrested* him."

"Do we know that for sure?" I argue. "I mean, yeah, there *was* a huge sign tacked on the cabin door from the freaking Sheriff of Nottingham, but my name was on there, and so was Chris's. And neither of *us* was arrested. What if my dad wasn't either?"

A heavy silence fills the tent.

"If that's the case," Chris says at last, "then your dad would find a way to get to you. He's that kind of man."

"What if he's dead?" I mutter, chilled.

"He's not dead." Chris shares a concerned glance with his mother. "Let's not talk about this now. You need to eat and get cleaned up. All of us do. It's been a long day."

Tell me about it. One of the longest days of my life.

And I thought standing in line at the DMV was a bad deal.

We eat a hot, heavy meal of canned meat, vegetables and bread. I devour everything, starving for big portions of food. I haven't seen Sophia since I arrived, but I'm betting she's doing the same thing as I am right now:

Stuffing her face.

When I'm done eating, I follow Mrs. Young to the back of the tent. She lifts up a small flap and we walk outside. There's a big metal bin sitting on the edge of the campsite, surrounded by several curtains made of tarpaulin. It's a makeshift washroom. "Jeff will get you some water, and you can start scrubbing away all of that dirt," she says.

I swipe my hand over my arm rub the crud between my thumb and index finger. Yeah. That's gross on a number of levels. Thanks for that, Kamaneva.

"Okay, here you go." Jeff comes around the corner about a half an hour later. I help him fill the tub with cool water. I'd prefer taking a bubble bath, but hey. This is better than nothing. He leaves me alone and I get an hour of something I haven't had in a long time: Privacy.

I peel off my prison-issued clothes and step into the water. It's cold, but it feels good. I scrub every inch of dirt and filth off my body. Mrs. Young brings me some clean clothes and she takes the old ones away.

She's probably going to burn them.

That's what *I'd* do.

When I'm done, I dress in snug cargo pants, a long sleeve shirt, a jacket and a pair of combat boots. I slip on socks and lace up the shoes, delighted to be reunited with some footwear that loves me as much as I love them.

"All right," I say, combing my fingers through my wet hair. "We're back in business."

When I step back into the tent, it's already getting dark. Chris looks up at me. He's clean. His black tee shirt is tight against his lean, muscular frame. His hair is hanging loose and damp around his face. I don't even realize I'm staring at him until he laughs.

"See something you like?" he teases.

"Um…" I blush. "I was just…you know…looking."

"I know." He stands up and places one hand on each side of my face. "You look beautiful when you're cleaned up."

I grin.

"As opposed to what? Looking like I was just liberated from enslavement?"

"Nah, you always look pretty." Chris presses a slow, gentle kiss against my lips. Enough to make my toes curl. "I'm sorry you had to go through this. It was my job to protect you, and I failed."

"You didn't fail at anything-"

"-Let me finish, Cassie." He pulls back and starts pacing. "I don't know if you've been impressed with the fact that I went crazy trying to find you. I looked *everywhere.*" He stops and takes a deep breath. "You scared the crap out of me."

I swallow.

"I'm sorry," I say.

"When I found out where you were through the Underground in the Free Army, I knew I had to come get you." He glances across the campsite where Max is gathered with a few of the men. "Max was instrumental. He did a lot behind the scenes to keep you alive. But when Kamaneva put you in solitary, he knew you were going to be executed the next morning. We had to change our plans. We had to attack the camp a lot earlier than we were thinking."

"You were amazing," I shrug. "You completely surprised Omega."

"We got lucky." He stops again. "You came way too close to getting killed. I owe everything to Max for saving you from that bullet."

"Max is a good man," I agree. "I can't believe I thought he was a sleazy creep who liked hitting on teenage girls."

Chris busts up laughing again.

"Max is an extremely talented actor," he says. "Probably the most talented guy in camp."

I look around, spotting Isabel's head of blonde hair near Mrs. Young.

"Isabel's happy here," I say.

"My parents have all but adopted her."

"Good. She needs parents." I look at Chris. "Can I ask you something?"

"Of course."

"Jeff said there was somebody named Alexander in charge before you came to camp. Who was he?"

"No one person was really in charge," he replies, playing with my fingers. "People were simply following Alexander's commands because he's a military guy and that was a lot better than sitting in the mud, wondering how to strike out at Omega."

"But then you came to camp and they fell in love with you," I joke. Only it's the truth. Chris has that effect on people. He's logical, smart, common sense. Roll all of these attributes into one and you've got yourself a popular leader.

"No, I just have a different approach than Ramos," Chris says.

"Ramos?"

"Ramos. Alexander Ramos."

I blink.

"So is he still in camp, then?"

"Yeah. He's a good soldier, he's just got an attitude."

I smirk.

"Like me?"

"No. Like an egotistical jerk." Chris gives me a *look*. "Stay away from him if you can avoid it. He's not a bad guy, but he's not a good guy, either. He can be...rough around the edges."

I slide to the ground and curl up on one of the camping mattresses.

"I guess that's your way of saying he's not a gentleman."

"Exactly." Chris ambles over and sits beside me, stroking my hair as I lay with my cheek pressed against a sleeping bag.

"This is a good group of fighting men, and their purpose is to create enough chaos to keep Omega from taking a deep hold here." He traces my ear with his fingertip, moving down to my neck. "But it's just like any other society. You have to watch your back. There will always be people who aren't as nice as you think they are. Ask anybody who's experienced any type of military environment and they'll tell you to keep your eyes open."

His fingers touch the gold chain hanging around my neck.

"You *kept* this?" he exclaims, surprised. "They didn't confiscate it?"

I smile up at him.

"I guess that's just God's way of winking at me." I touch his hand. "You know, when I was in that place, and they were killing people on the sidewalk, and Kamaneva was making us march through the locker rooms naked, I kept thinking about something."

Chris's jaw hardens.

"I swear, if I could kill-"

"-Don't you want to know what I was thinking about?" I interrupt, feigning disappointment.

Chris visibly relaxes.

"Okay. Shoot."

"I was thinking about *you*." I press my lips against the center of his forehead. "I kept asking myself what *you* would do in my situation. And I knew you'd come for me – and you did." I slide my arms around his neck. "Thank you, Chris."

I'm so close to him that I can hear the rapid beat of his heart. He gently lays me back onto the sleeping bag and gives me a kiss. "You make it easy," he whispers.

I fold myself against his chest, feeling completely secure in his embrace. Nothing and nobody can come between us now. Exhaustion, starvation, trauma – whatever it is that's eating at my nerves – melts away. I close my eyes and, for the first time in a very long time, I sleep peacefully.

Yeah. Thanks Chris.

What would I do without you?

Now that I'm done hibernating, I feel like a new person. It's amazing what a little food and water can do. To say nothing of clean clothes, an environment that's not bloodthirsty, and fresh mountain air.

Oh, and then there's Chris.

Did I mention him? I guess I did. I think I love him.

I've been sleeping on and off for three days. The exhaustion of slave labor finally caught up with me, and after the much needed downtime, I've got my energy back. Cassidy Hart has returned, people. And this time around, there's no cruel, mouthy Russian woman to push her around.

Chalk one point up to my team, please.

Today is the first day I've felt like exploring the campsite, and as I do, I learn a lot about the Free Army. There are elderly couples, singles, children and families here. Everyone contributes to the maintenance and survival of the community as a whole. Women and men share an equal work burden. The women keep the supplies organized and make sure the food is used in a way that will feed the most mouths. Men constantly scout the area, and there are guards posted around the campsite at all times. All the while, Chris is taking the liberated prisoners from the labor camp and turning them into new recruits.

Sophia and I are sitting on a fallen log, watching him talk to them. Both men and women are wearing clean clothes. Like me, they're so happy to be freed from enslavement that the idea of joining an army seems like a great opportunity.

And, also like me, they might change their mind later.

"You know what I think?" Sophia says.

"Hmm?"

"I think Chris Young is way too old for you."

"Age is but a number."

"Yeah, but he's a lot different than you are. I mean, he's all logical and mature and you're…"

"I'm what? Illogical and scatterbrained?"

Sophia giggles.

"No," she says. "I just mean…you're *different.*"

"True. But we're the same, too." I pick at a loose thread on my pants. "Look what he did to save me. He took command of an *army*. How many guys would do that?"

"Good point. He must really love you."

I lick my lips.

I've never heard Chris say those three words to me before, but…that doesn't mean he doesn't love me. I think it's obvious by the way he protects me that there's more to this than a simple crush.

"Shall we join the army today then?" I ask Sophia.

She shakes her head. Her dark skin is a stark contrast to the green tee shirt she's wearing. She's got the kind of exotic beauty I always dreamed about. But really, who cares about stuff like that anymore? Being pretty isn't going to keep my butt out of Omega's crosshairs.

"Tomorrow. Let's watch today," she replies.

"Okay."

Chris is launching into a lecture. I'm starting to wonder if he's got a list of inspirational speeches memorized. He's talking about the kind of commitment it's going to take for the new recruits to join the Free Army.

"It won't be easy," he says. "In fact, it's going to be the most challenging thing you've ever done. You're going to want to quit. You're going to want to surrender. You're going to want all of this to disappear." He pauses, stretching the moment. The crowd is hanging on every word that comes out of his mouth. "But in the end it's going to be worth it, because Omega can't be everywhere at once. Our job is to create enough chaos to make them want to leave our homes alone. We're not a big enough militia force to meet them on an open battlefield. We don't have the manpower or the firepower for that. What we *do* have is strategy, and something to fight for. This is *our* home, and you have to decide if you're willing to sacrifice everything to take it back from Omega."

He stops and clasps his hands behind his back, instructor-style.

"Can you commit?"

There's a dead silence. Isabel clambers across the log and squeezes me into a playful hug, her eyes on the conversation going down in front of us. At last, somebody in line steps forward. "I can commit," he says. He's a tall, lean young man. A rifle is slung across his back.

"What's your name?" Chris asks.

"Andrew," he replies. "And I'm in."

Chris nods approvingly.

A few other guys step forward and, after several moments, the entire crowd of ex-POWs takes one step, signifying their decision. My chest swells with pride – pride for Chris's leadership, pride for the people willing to give their lives to take down Omega.

It's a rush.

"Thank you," Chris says, rubbing his chin. "My men and I will begin training you. It won't be long before you'll be able to inflict as much damage on Omega as they've inflicted on us. It won't take much to turn all of you into their worst nightmare."

After a few more minutes of talking, Chris lets another man speak. I don't recognize him. He's tall, blonde and blue eyed. Young. His plaid button up is tucked into his blue jeans.

Chris looks at me, ghosting a smile.

"He's got it bad for you," Sophia grins.

I feel warm.

"The feeling's mutual."

"You'd be crazy if it wasn't."

The blonde guy wraps up his talk, and then Chris is moving the group away from camp. I'm assuming they're going somewhere to train. I stand up and stretch.

"We should train, too," I say. "I want to help."

"Me too!" Isabel is walking back and forth on the log, balancing like a tightrope walker. "Chris says nobody's too young or old to help win this war."

Sophia winces at the word *war*. I don't blame her. It's a loaded word.

Small, but loaded.

"I'm going to grab lunch," Sophia says. "Mrs. Young is making something. I can see her from here."

"I'm coming with you," Isabel replies, jumping off the log and taking Sophia's hand. The two of them have become pretty close in the last few days. "Coming, Cassie?"

"Yeah, I'll be right there."

Something catches my attention at the other side of camp. Sophia and Isabel walk towards the Young's tent. I head in the opposite direction. A tall, powerful man with dark, cropped hair is standing with his arms crossed. He's studying me. Judging by his appearance, I'm going to make an assumption: he's ex-military. He *has* to be with his build, hairstyle and presence.

"Hey," I say, approaching.

He cocks an eyebrow.

"I'm Cassidy," I continue. "Are you helping Chris train the recruits?"

He shifts his stance, giving me a cold once-over.

"Ramos," he replies, his voice gravelly. A smoker's voice. "Alexander Ramos."

"I know who you are." I stop myself. "I mean, yeah. I heard about you."

"Really?" He smells like smoke.

He pops a package of cigarettes out of his pocket.

"Smoke?" he asks.

"No thanks." I watch him take a cigarette out. Light it. "Where do you get those? I don't think they're selling them at the local gas station these days."

Alexander snorts.

"A lot of people leave them behind in their houses," he says.

I notice the lines around his mouth.

"Well, I just wanted to...introduce myself," I say lamely.

I turn to leave, but he catches my shoulder.

His hands are huge – almost three times the size of mine.

"Cassidy," he says, narrowing his eyes.

I take a step backwards under the intensity of his gaze.

"Yeah?"

"Be careful," he warns.

"Careful?"

He takes a long drag. Then he stalks off as if I never existed, leaving me alone on the edge of camp.

I shrug off his strange behavior as the attitude problem Chris was talking about and head back to the Young family tent. Mrs. Young has cooked up some lunch, and it smells delicious. I'm surprised Omega can't track us down based on the scent of our campfire cooking alone.

"You know, Chris was telling me that you thought your father might have been taken to the city as a war criminal," Mrs. Young says, setting a bowl down in front of me. "But after what I've seen of Omega, I don't think they'd bother."

She makes an attempt to smooth back her wispy gray hair as she sits down and joins Sophia, Isabel and myself at a table. "What makes you say that?" I ask.

"Because Omega doesn't just single people out of the crowd," Mrs. Young says, "unless they have a very good reason. As far as I know, your father just got caught in the wrong place at the wrong time."

"They made a point of leaving the warrant of arrest up for everybody to see," I answer. "Why would they do that if they didn't think he was important enough to single out?"

"Your father sounds like a smart man, from what you've told me," Mrs. Young continues. "And I could be very wrong, Cassidy, but I feel like Omega wouldn't waste their time taking war criminals back to the cities."

"Why wouldn't they?" Sophia asks.

"There's nothing left of the cities," Mrs. Young says, stirring her bowl of soup. "Rumor is, Los Angeles was attacked with a chemical weapon not long after the EMP. I've heard from other people in camp that a *lot* of the major cities in the country were destroyed with a chemical weapon, too."

Sophia stops eating. The color drains from her cheeks.

"I thought New York was nuked."

"There are those rumors, too." Mrs. Young studies the branches of the trees before she goes on. "I don't know a lot about military strategy like my sons, but if I was an invading army, I would want to take over everything – not destroy it and rebuild it. If it's already in place, why waste all that time building everything from scratch?"

"A chemical weapon would wipe out the population," I say, realization dawning, "but it would leave the infrastructure of the city in place. Omega could literally clean out the dead people and then move in."

Sophia covers her mouth.

"That's *disgusting*!"

"It could be exactly what happened." I fold my hands together. "You might be right."

Then what *did* happen to my dad?

Did Omega arrest him and send him to a labor camp? Was he killed on sight? I have no idea, and I'm afraid that if I spend too much time thinking about it, I'll go crazy.

So I focus on something else.

"Who do you think Omega is?" I ask.

"An alliance." Mrs. Young doesn't hesitate with her answer. "We know Russia is involved. Alexander is from the Midwest. He said he suspected Syria and North Korea were involved as well. There could be more."

"Well, *somebody* decided to gang up on us," I sigh. "How nice."

After we finish lunch, I decide to go for a stroll around the campsite. My strength has returned and I want to familiarize myself with everything before I begin training with the rest of the recruits. Then again, thinking of myself as a "recruit" is a new train of thought entirely.

I was never the type of person who engaged in strenuous physical activity outside of jogging, hiking or riding a bicycle. And suddenly I'm going to join a guerilla militia group and fight against an invading army?

God has a great sense of humor.

On the east edge of the camp, a few guards are stationed around the perimeter. Many of them are hidden in the forest a good distance away from the camp, just in case someone tries to sneak up on us. It's always good to be prepared.

As that thought crosses my mind, Harry pops out of the bushes. He's wearing combat pants and a sizable walking stick.

"Um..." I say. "What are you doing out here?"

He draws back, clutching his weapon, and drops his eyes.

"Guarding," he replies.

"What's with the stick?"

"I'm not allowed to have a gun," he states sourly.

Gee, I wonder why.

"Look, Harry," I begin. "I know you didn't set me up on purpose. Kamaneva was an evil woman. I was angry with you at first, but I'm not anymore. I understand why you did what you did. I forgive you."

Forgiveness is not something I dole out on a regular basis. In fact, I have been known to hold a grudge against late postal carriers and waitresses who forget to put lemon in my water. But this is different. Harry didn't betray me because he's a bad person. He betrayed me because *Kamaneva* was.

"I should have been stronger," he replies, exhaling. "I should have refused. That's what your boyfriend would have done."

"You were scared. It's okay."

"Well, there comes a point when you've just got to look after your own skin," he snaps, glaring at me. Mood swing alert. "That's what I was doing. Any logical person would have done the same thing."

One second he's apologizing and the next he's making excuses for himself. I don't understand him.

"Forget it," I sigh. "I just wanted you to know that I'm not angry with you."

"Bloody likely," he mutters.

"Whatever. Be that way."

I leave, upset. I've never had anybody reject mercy before. Is that even possible? If I did something bad, I'd want somebody's forgiveness...wouldn't I? Maybe it's just a pride thing. Harry's obviously embarrassed that he sold me out to Kamaneva.

He'll get over it.

If I can, he can, too.

Chapter Ten

Rest and relaxation can only last so long before A) something goes wrong or B) you have to get back to work. I consider life one big long list of As, but today is an exception. It's time to get back to work.

The liberated prisoners are being turned into a guerilla war-fighting group to be reckoned with. The militiamen are training them every day – hard. As a result, the Free Army has dozens of new citizen soldiers, both young and old. And Sophia and I are among the newest recruits.

Chris, because of his natural leadership abilities, has grown to become the leader of our militia. People look up to him. Ever since the raid on the labor camp came off successfully, nobody's even questioned the idea that Chris should be in charge. Below Chris, there are other men who instruct the newbies. The first one is Alexander Ramos. Tall, tanned, slightly anti-social. Chris told me that he was an active-duty Recon Marine home on leave when the world went haywire. Aside from that, no one knows much about him. He's a man of mystery, and despite his gruff exterior, Chris seems to trust him.

Next we've got Max. Outside of his Omega uniform, he looks like a different person. No more Grease. His hair is cut short and the fine features of his face stand out against his brown eyes. He can't be older than thirty.

We have a young man named Derek. About twenty-three years old, he's got short blond hair and a tall, powerful frame.

He'd only been in the military for a year before the EMP hit. An explosives specialist in the Army.

And then there's me. I'm not an instructor. Heck, I don't even know if I count as a student. But I'm here. I want to do everything I can to help this group – I owe them that much for rescuing me from prison. Besides, with no clue where my dad is, what choice do I have but to keep busy? If I sit around and think about all of the things I've lost since the EMP, I'll turn into a delusional downer.

Kind of like Harry.

One of the first things Chris wants the new recruits to learn is how to handle a weapon. An army is useless without weapons, and since Omega is equipped with guns and bombs, it's only fair that we fight fire with fire. The militia has amassed stockpiles of weaponry from Omega storehouse raids, abandoned houses and other sources. Chris starts off newbies like me at the very bottom. My knowledge of weaponry is limited to what my father showed me when I was in high school. And most of that consisted of,

"Do *this* if you're attacked in a dark parking lot, then run like hell and call 911."

There's no 911 anymore. I'll have to think outside the box.

We start day one with something I like to call the "Dummy Course." Chris and the other instructors roll out rugs and mats along the edge of camp and nail targets to trees. We're given an empty, harmless rifle and told to lie facedown on the rugs.

I settle onto the rug and prop myself up on my elbows, watching Chris assess the line of trainees. His lips twitch in an obvious attempt to abstain from laughter.

We must look pretty bad.

"Form good habits now," Chris says, "and you'll make active combat a lot easier for yourself and your team. You actually have an advantage if you're completely new to this. You haven't had the time to form bad habits, so everything you learn now will be the *right* way. You won't have to unlearn bad habits." He stops at the end of the line and kneels next to me. "I want you to learn how to shoot straight and steady," he says. "Omega's got numbers and firepower, but if we make every single bullet count, we can even out the playing field. We'll be neat where they're sloppy and we'll be fast where they're slow."

He positions my left hand under the barrel of the rifle, bringing the stock into my shoulder. "Bring your right knee up," he says. "Let your body relax."

"I *am* relaxed."

I crane my neck to the right to try to see down the sights of the rifle. Chris places his hands on my head, moving it to a more natural position. "Don't do that," he instructs. "Just fall into it. Find the natural place for your cheek to rest against the stock of the weapon."

"I can't see through the sights if I don't tilt my head."

"Yes, you can. If you're in the natural position everything will be easier."

I try. It takes me a couple of hours to get the hang of it, and I'm not the only one who's having issues. Sophia is having trouble learning the stances and positions. I tease her about it – until I have to do the same thing.

It's not as easy as it looks.

In fact, it's not easy *period*.

After we learn the basics, we're shown how to shoot standing up. This is a lot harder for me. The guns are heavy, nearly as big as I am. Chris shows me how to use the rifle sling to take the weight off my arms, which helps, but thanks to weeks of manual labor under Kamaneva's command, my arms are a lot stronger than they look and I adjust quickly.

For two days, this is all we do. We run through basic drills over and over with unloaded weapons. Alexander Ramos gives long, detailed lectures about guerilla war fighting techniques, drawing in the dirt to illustrate his points. Chris shows us how to use the features of the terrain around us to our advantage, like hiding in plain sight or firing from cover. Max lectures us on Omega inside secrets. Their routines, their chain of command, their fighting methods.

Yet through it all, there's a constant theme: simplicity. We're learning to keep things simple, quick and lethal. We have to. Omega is way bigger than us, and the only way we'll stand a chance against them is if our little army is better organized than theirs. Hit hard, hit fast, and get out. It's really no different than the guerilla techniques used centuries ago during the Revolutionary War.

On the third day, Chris lets us shoot. We apply all of the techniques we've learned and set our sights on various targets at different distances. Chris doesn't want us to blow through too much ammunition, so our practice with live fire is limited. But it's okay. Some of us are hitting accurately enough to kill an Omega soldier up to four hundred yards away. Even *I'm* getting good at this, which is an amazing accomplishment in itself. Chris has noticed my skills improving, and he continually makes comments like, "Nice work, Cassie," or "Good job."

In Chris talk that means:

"Wow. I'm very impressed."

At the end of the week, Chris and the other militiamen in charge seem satisfied with our progress. Personally, I'm impressed with how far we've come in such a short amount of time. A week ago I couldn't put a magazine into a rifle without guidance. Now I can do it with my eyes closed.

"I feel so hardcore," I remark, sitting cross-legged next to Sophia. We're eating lunch. It's a warm day. The sun is filtering through the tree branches, reminding us that it's almost April.

"How so?" Sophia asks.

"Oh, you know. Joining the army kind of gave me a confidence boost."

She laughs, but a few seconds later she turns her head.

"Harry," she hisses from the side of her mouth.

I look over my shoulder. He's sitting alone on the edge of camp, stabbing his food with a camping spork. He's also glaring in our direction. Part of me wants to go over and start a conversation with the guy – he's obviously lonely. But common sense tells me that it would be a waste of time. Nobody is making Harry sit in the corner of camp, and nobody is shunning him, either. If anything, he's shunning *us.*

"He's bitter, isn't he?" Sophia comments.

"Seems to be." I shrug. "I think he's mad at himself for screwing up. And I think he's terrified of Chris, which is understandable. I'd be scared of him too if I was Harry."

"Still...Harry's weird."

I return my attention to my lunch. Harry's not really weird. He's just...confused.

"Mind if I join you, ladies?" a gruff voice rumbles.

I look up, meeting the gaze of Alexander Ramos. I'm too stunned to say anything. He hasn't spoken directly to me since the day I met him – and that was an odd encounter.

"You're doing well," he says, sitting in a vacant chair.

"Excuse me?"

"In your training. You've advanced fast." Alexander folds his hands together. "Both of you have."

Sophia blushes. It makes me want to gag. Lately she's been nursing an ill-concealed crush on Alexander, one that I keep trying to discourage. True, I don't have any real reason to *not* like the man. I just trust Chris when he says that he doesn't think Alexander is completely stable.

Then again, Chris seems to trust him to an extent.

Hypocrisy in the workplace.

"You've got talent," he continues, looking right at me. "And you should utilize it. Chris is going to try to hold you back because he wants to keep you safe. Don't let that happen."

I bristle at the suggestion that Chris would do that.

"I don't know how he would hold me back," I say.

"Easy. He'll put you in positions where you can't get hurt. Where you won't be used to your full potential." He leans forward. "Don't let him do that to you. We need everybody's talent on the line, here. You're quick with your hands and your feet. You're a good shot. We can use you."

He takes a long breath, reaching for a cigarette.

How many of those does he have?

"Thanks for the advice," I say, uninspired.

"Don't mention it." He stands up, dusting his pants off. "Like I said before, be careful."

"I don't know what that means."

"Just don't let yourself be pushed aside. That goes for you too, Rodriguez."

Sophia perks up when he mentions her last name. He walks away, flipping a lighter out of his pocket. I make a face and return to my meal.

"He's handsome," she sighs.

"He's strange." I brush my bangs out of my eyes. "I don't know why he felt the need to tell us that. It doesn't even make sense."

"Maybe he's just a nice guy who's concerned about us."

"Maybe...he *was* in charge until Chris came around." I tilt my head back and try to put myself in his shoes. "If I were him, I'd probably be a little upset about it."

Sophia ignores me.

We the eat the rest of our lunch in silence, thinking about our training, thinking about Alexander Ramos, thinking about poor, cowardly Harry. When we're done, we join the other recruits for more training. I find myself zoning out and struggling to stay awake as the warm afternoon daylight hits my face.

"Can you believe it?" Sophia whispers.

"Hmm?"

I blink a few times, lifting my drowsy head, focusing in on Chris's figure standing over me. He's looking at me with an expression of wry amusement – or annoyance.

Probably the latter.

"What?" I say, stifling a yawn.

"Weren't you paying attention?" he asks.

"Yes. Kind of."

"Chris said we're going to hit Omega for real this time."

He has my full attention now.

"Are you sure?" I ask.

"You're ready," Chris says, looking at me, then focusing on something in the distance. "You need firsthand experience."

But I can tell by the look on his face and the tone of his voice that he's not taking this lightly. Good. Because neither am I.

Are we ready for this?

Ready or not, here we come. That's our motto for the next few hours. Chris is standing next to me on the edge of camp, cinching up his boots, rechecking his gear. The sky is dark, broken only by starlight filtering through the clouds. I'm standing here, twiddling my thumbs, full of nervous energy as I get my gear together in the near darkness of the forest. Rifle? Check. Sling? Double check. Shoelaces tied? Make that a triple check, and just to be on the safe side, I'll throw in a double knot. Jeff's knife is strapped around my thigh. It's always been something of a good luck charm to me in the past, so I like to keep it with me.

Chris straightens up and places his hands on my shoulders. With his black clothing, he blends into the shadows around the campsite.

"Don't be nervous," he says. "I'll be with you."

"You can't stick with me all the time," I reply. "You've got a militia to lead. Don't worry about me."

"I'll worry about you if I want to."

He pulls me into a gentle kiss. I melt into him, desperate to touch him. I feel like this is some kind of goodbye.

That's irrational, I tell myself. *We'll be back in no time.*

But this is war. Anything can happen.

Across the camp, the muted shadow of Alexander Ramos is standing still, his arms folded across his chest, watching us. As Chris wraps his arms around me for a final, comforting hug, I place my head against his chest and watch him.

Don't let yourself be pushed aside, he said.

Stupid advice. Chris isn't afraid of letting me help.

"Stick to the plan and follow orders," Chris says, "and you'll be fine. Don't deviate. If things go bad, head to the rally point where the vehicles will be. You can't mess around and wing it, Cassie. This is life or death."

I nod.

"Yes, sir."

He smiles softly, tucking a loose strand of hair behind my ear. The militia hasn't made a move against Omega since Chris and his group attacked the labor camp. This will be the first mission we've attempted since the liberated prisoners became new recruits over the last few weeks. Our target is an Omega supply depot in Squaw Valley.

"Omega is using people like you and me to farm the land and collect the supplies," Chris says, gathering the militia around the center of camp. We're dressed in dark clothes, blending in with the night. "They're an invading army, and we can surmise that they're an advance force prepping for the next wave of troops to come in, so they need our food to keep going. Not to mention our labor. So what we need to do is make it impossible for Omega to stay here by taking away what they need, and making sure any new forces in the area don't have a reason to settle in. The best way to do this is to cut off their supply chain. We start by liberating the POWs and taking back the food supplies. Just like we've done in the past, but on a larger scale." He takes a step back, locking gazes with me for a moment. "We're not training anymore. This is real. You get one chance to do your job right, and if you hesitate, there's a very real chance that you will endanger the mission or get yourself killed. It's important that you follow orders. Focus on the objective. Continually keep the enemy reacting to *our* actions. This will keep you and your friends alive."

He pauses.

"But the best soldier is the one who can improvise," he continues. "There will be instances in which my orders do not fit with a given situation. You'll be forced to make a tough decision. Think on your feet and do what you know is right. We can't afford to take many losses. Every man counts. Take the road that will get as many of you out of that situation alive. Keep your group together and make sure you maintain communication with the members of your team.

"A battlefield is loud and chaotic, and it's easy to get separated. Do exactly as you've been trained. Shoot, move, and communicate. Fighting rarely goes as planned, so yes, follow orders, but be prepared to adapt, improvise and overcome when things get hard." He folds his arms across his chest, keeping his gaze steady. "We'll be separated into four platoons. Each platoon will take one side of the depot, surrounding it on all sides. Only two platoons will attack at a time. Omega will turn to respond with fire, and then our next two platoons will open fire from the other side, as we discussed in training. It will keep them guessing. Our most powerful weapon tonight will be the element of surprise. Max and his team will be in charge of opening the gate for us."

The men chuckle. Max's team is comprised of demolition experts and men who know how to make things go boom in a major way.

"While our three platoons are surrounding the depot," Chris finishes, "Max's team will be maneuvering to breach the front gate with explosives, essentially giving us a way to enter the property. We should be able to pin Omega's forces against the rear concrete wall. They'll be trapped. Nowhere to run."

The Omega center in Squaw Valley is a giant warehouse. It's small in comparison to the one I was imprisoned in, but it's a good place for a small, fledgling fighting group like us to start.

Sophia gives my hand a reassuring squeeze before we separate into our platoons. There are four: Max, Alexander, Derek and Chris. Since my skillset is primarily marksmanship, I'm with Chris's group. He's leading us around the front end of the warehouse. Sophia is with Alexander Ramos's team. Her platoon will round the back of the depot and focus on closer targets.

Each group is assigned a truck. I sit with Chris in the cab of ours, while the rest of our team piles into the back. My heart is racing. We've gone over our training a thousand times. I should be able to do this. But I'm still scared. No amount of training will ever change the fact that deep down, I'm just a teenage girl from L.A. who got kicked into a war zone.

Chris starts the engine and we take off, driving down the mountain roads. Luckily, the moon is bright tonight, making it easy to navigate the roads without headlights. We stick to bumpy back roads that cut behind the main highways – roads that are far away from the routine Omega patrols. The supply center we're hitting is about an hour away from our camp, but it will take longer to get there since we have to go slow – a necessary precaution to keep the engine noise to a minimum.

"Don't drive fast or anything," I mutter.

Chris simply smiles, but it's a tight smile. Just because he's a leader these days doesn't mean he's impervious to fear or nerves. I sometimes forget that he's human, too.

"We'll be okay," I say, keeping my voice light.

"I know." He keeps his eyes trained on the road. "Maybe you should have stayed with my parents back at camp."

"Why?"

"I don't want you to get hurt."

"I'm *fine.*" I fold my arms across my chest. "I'm just as capable or talented as any of the other recruits around here."

"I didn't say you weren't capable or talented." He sighs. "I just said I don't want you to get hurt."

"I won't."

A heavy silence hangs between us.

"Cassie, I came too close to losing you before," he says at last.

"Chris, you don't-"

"-Just hear me out." He throws a glance in my direction. "I don't want you to feel like you have to do this with me. If you feel like you're not ready, or if you'd rather stay back at camp, you can tell me."

I place my right hand around the car door handle.

"Believe me, I'd tell you," I reply. "Don't worry."

I take a deep, steadying breath. Chris has every right to be cautious when it comes to me jumping headfirst into a battle. How many times have I almost died in the last few months? How many times has he had to save my sorry butt, too?

Yeah, I can see his point.

But I can't spend the rest of my life hiding in the foothills. I have to do my part to stop Omega, and after being imprisoned – and almost executed – I feel a personal desire to take them out.

Call it revenge. Call it whatever you want to call it.

I'm obligated.

Chris doesn't say anything for the rest of the drive. We travel in silence, wrapped up in our own thoughts. The tension is thick. We finally arrive at our destination, a small clearing in the middle of the forest a few miles away from the supply depot. We need to be far enough away from the compound so we can have the element of surprise.

This will also be our primary rally point if something goes wrong.

"Let's go," Chris says.

I nod.

He catches my chin between his fingers, pressing a kiss against my lips.

"Cassie, I..." He shakes his head. "Just be careful and stay close to me."

"Will do."

My heart twists a little in my chest.

We get out of the truck. We're about a half a mile away from the supply center. Nobody speaks. Nobody breathes. We fall into our platoons like we planned, keeping everything silent and efficient.

I stay close to Chris's shoulder as our platoon separates into the woods. The foothills are bright and beautiful in the moonlight, making it simple to navigate the path – but easier for Omega to see us coming if we're not careful. In the distance, I spot the supply center. It's an old warehouse surrounded by a parking lot. Omega trucks are parked there, and a big barbed wire fence has been erected around the perimeter. In the back, a cinderblock fence is lined with wiring around the top.

Looks familiar.

Troopers are guarding a few smaller buildings next to the main warehouse. That's where they're keeping the POWs. Chris crouches down and we follow suit, lying prone, watching the buildings through the tall grass. Chris has his binoculars trained on the front entrance. The other three platoons are closing in on the warehouse, and pretty soon we'll have it surrounded on all sides.

"I really hope they don't have satellite cameras," I whisper.

"Nobody has satellite surveillance anymore," somebody says behind me.

"I'll bet Omega does."

I mean, why not? They've got working cars, don't they? They've got generators. They might as well have their own satellite. Unfortunately, the thought that we could be watched from the sky is enough to make my nervousness skyrocket.

Relax. Breathe. Just stay calm.

I can never get my body to cooperate with me when I want it to. And right now, all I want it to do is relax. My hands are shaking and my shoulders are trembling. The cold temperature is making it worse, too.

Chris takes my hand.

"Hey," he whispers. "We got this."

I force a smile.

And just a second ago I was the one calming *his* nerves.

We move closer to the building. As we approach, I can see that it used to be some sort of big repair shop, but Omega has, once again, commandeered something good and turned it into something bad. It makes me sick – and it reminds me why I'm here.

Just stay focused, I think. *Don't do anything stupid.*

When we're as close as we can get, we drop to into the prone position again. Our weapons are at the ready. I lay mine across a log to take the weight off my arm. It will make my aim steadier. Our goal is to wait for Alexander's team and Derek's team to maneuver into place while Max and his men set up the fireworks.

Several tense minutes pass before Chris finally says, "Now." We can't see the other platoons. We can only go by time – and hope that everyone does their job according to the plan. There are at least ten troopers standing guard on this side of the supply building. Two inside the fence, two outside the fence at the entrance, three around the warehouse itself and two more patrolling the front of the storage buildings being used to house prisoners. We're close enough to see the white O stitched into their uniform sleeve. Close enough to hear their conversations.

Close enough to take them out.

Chris gives the signal for us to open fire by taking the first shot. It's perfect. A trooper drops dead at the front entrance. As he does, our group starts firing from the cover of the grass and the trees, and more troopers fall. When Omega finally starts regrouping and hitting us with return fire, we drop into the grass. The other two platoons open fire, shooting at Omega from the opposite side. Omega scrambles to get it together, but it's not happening. This goes on for a while. We trade off coordinated volleys until Omega's numbers are significantly reduced. Shoot, drop, let the other side pummel Omega while we reload. Rise up again, shoot, drop. Rinse and repeat. Omega troopers keep falling. Our numbers remain the same.

One or two desperate troopers duck for cover and yell for backup, but as they do, the main gate explodes. Just like it did at Kamaneva's camp – only now I recognize the militiamen's handiwork.

I duck my head as the explosion sends a wave of heat over our hiding place. I keep my weapon aimed at the entrance, sweeping back and forth, looking for an Omega trooper that might appear in my sights.

The explosion at the front entrance lights up the property and gives us access to the grounds. Omega troopers are scrambling, trying to figure out what the heck is going on. It's like the rescue at the labor camp all over again – only this time, I'm on the other side of the fence.

Chris gives the signal. He takes half of our group and bounds towards the building, leaving me and a few other militiamen behind to cover them. I watch them storm the camp along with Alexander, Derek and Max, systematically taking out Omega's lines of defense. If anything, they make it look too easy.

But I know better.

Chris is just *that* good.

Omega troopers run from the building, attempting to stop the militiamen from rushing the camp, but there's not a lot they can do. Our forces are already inside. Explosions rock the ground like thunder. Gunfire rips the air. Yelling, screaming. Fire, smoke, heat. It takes every ounce of self-restraint in my body to stay on the ground and not run after Chris to try to help him.

But this is the new me.

I actually do what I'm told.

As I watch the scene unfold, I notice an Omega trooper coming around the corner of the big warehouse. He's armed and, because of the thick smoke, hard to see. He shoots one of our men. I suck in my breath, dropping my head, looking down my sights. I don't even think about what I do next. I just aim, squeeze, and shoot. He's at least two hundred yards away, but it's a good shot. He drops instantly as my bullet hits him right in the chest.

I release a breath and close my eyes.

Somebody – I don't know who – claps me on the back and says something congratulatory. A sick feeling pools in my stomach and I fight the urge to gag. I intentionally killed someone. Granted, I did it to keep *him* from killing someone *else*, but still.

The realization hits hard.

There's no time to feel guilty. Everything's moving fast. Alexander reaches the entrance and gives the all-clear signal, and the rest of us jump to our feet and storm the camp with the remainder of our forces. Omega is overrun, dropping their weapons, throwing their hands in the air. I enter the property with my weapon raised, the stench of burning metal and gunpowder singeing my lungs.

"Cassie, stay behind cover!" Chris yells, appearing from the smoke. He grabs my arm and pulls me behind the corner of the warehouse. "Stay out of the open." He pauses, looking at the Omega trooper on the ground. "Nice shot."

His gaze falls to the other side of the camp, and his features harden. Alexander is rushing the last of Omega's defense with all of his troops. I watch three militiamen get shot and killed in the process. We can't afford those kinds of losses.

"Stay here," he orders.

Something about his tone screams danger. I stay behind the corner of the warehouse and watch as he makes his way across the parking lot, weaving through the battle zone like a boss. Derek cuts through the property, guns blazing, a feverish glint in his eyes. He seems to be enjoying this. Max takes off after Chris.

I watch them. What's wrong? What's the issue?

"Sophia!" I yell, waving her down.

Her head pops up and she runs over, clad in black. She's sweating. Besides the trail of blood running down her cheek, she looks unhurt. "Are you okay?" she asks, breathing hard.

"Yeah, fine. You?"

"Good. Something's going on with Ramos, though."

Something slams into my right shoulder, smashing me against the warehouse wall. I see stars and lose my balance, falling to the side. Sophia yells something and I hear a loud thud. I scramble to my feet, an Omega trooper right above us. He's using the stock of his rifle to attack us, which means he must be out of ammo. Blood and soot is smeared across his face.

I roll out of the way, narrowly avoiding a painful encounter with his boot. By the time I manage to climb to my feet, he's already attacking Sophia. I slam the stock of my own weapon into the back of his neck. He screams and stumbles, hitting the warehouse. I hit him again and, as he falls, Sophia plants a deadly kick to his head. He goes limp.

"Dead?" Sophia breathes.

"Unconscious."

Panting, I kneel down and dig through his pockets. Nothing. I turn my attention to the far side of camp. Chris is fighting side by side with Alexander. Max is doing the same and it looks like Derek is joining in.

"We should help," I say.

"I don't know."

As we speak, liberated prisoners begin running out of the containment units. There can't be more than fifty people, but it's enough. They overwhelm what's left of Omega's defense, making our job a lot easier. No more than ten minutes later, the supply center is nothing but a smoking memorial to Omega's degrading labor camp. Their men are either dead or disappeared – most of them fallen. Burning embers are littered across the ground. Ashes fall from the sky, coating my hair and skin. Dead troopers are everywhere. Several of our own militiamen are sprawled on the asphalt lot at unnatural angles. Fiery blazes spread across the edges of the property, crawling towards the buildings.

I bend down and gag, overwhelmed with the stench of burning flesh and human blood. My vision blurs with tears. *This* is the reality of war. Horrible killing.

Chris walks towards me through the smoke, his face covered with black smudge marks and sweat. He kneels beside me and places an arm around my shoulders. "You did good, kid," he says, pressing his lips against my temple. "I'm proud of you."

I cling to his arm as we stand together. Refugees are piling into commandeered Omega pickups as fast as they can. Supplies are being stuffed in with them, to be packed into our own vehicles back at the rally point. Militiamen are planting more explosives around the buildings. They'll detonate as we leave – which needs to be soon if we want to make a clean exit before Omega brings in backup.

"I had it!" Alexander growls from behind us.

His expression is lethal.

Chris keeps his arm around me, undeterred.

"We'll talk later," he states. "Get in the truck."

The veins are bulging in Alexander's neck. He's furious. I watch as he stalks away towards the truck. Chris's grip on me is unbreakable as he leads me back towards another truck.

"What was that all about?" I croak, my throat dry from the smoke.

"Nothing. Don't worry about it."

"Don't lie to me, Chris."

"I'm not." He opens the car door. "I'll tell you later," he promises. "Good job."

I crawl across the seat and settle down in the passenger side of the cab, kicking out trash and empty water bottles. By the time Chris jumps in the truck and revs the engine, we've got at least seven new vehicles, half of those loaded with fuel and food. It's an epic win. Chris floors it, and as we hit the road, the explosives detonate, turning what's left of the property into smoking ruins. I hold my head in my hands, bracing myself for the aftershock of emotions that will come once the adrenaline rush wears off.

Tonight we sent a message to Omega:

The hunted have become the hunters.

Chapter Eleven

Coming back to camp is like returning home from deployment. Granted, our deployment only lasted a few hours, but you get the point.

The Young family and Isabel are waiting for us, along with other members of the militia who stayed behind to guard the camp. Adrenaline is still simmering in my blood, keeping my senses sharp.

It will wear off soon.

When our truck pulls into camp, a pickup screeches up beside us. Alexander kills the engine on his pickup and storms out of his vehicle, slamming the door behind him. He stalks around the front of our truck and confronts Chris. I scramble out of the car and run around the back of the pickup bed just as Chris steps out of the vehicle.

"Why did you do that?" Alexander demands. "I had the situation under control!"

The other pickups are pulling into camp. The militiamen are high on victory, laughing and grinning. A sudden hush falls over the crowd as they notice the confrontation going down between Chris and Alexander.

"You had a situation," Chris replies calmly, "but you didn't have it under control."

"What was all that crap about 'the best soldier can improvise?'" Alexander hisses, getting in Chris's face. "I improvised, Young, and you screwed it up."

"You were making a mistake." Chris crosses his arms. "Go see to your men. We'll discuss this later when we debrief."

Little Isabel pokes her face out of the crowd and runs towards me, wrapping her arms around my waist in a hug. I kiss the top of her head, holding my breath.

"I won't forget this," Alexander warns, rolling his shoulders back.

"Good. Don't." Chris closes the pickup door. "And one more thing."

Alexander raises his eyebrows.

"Don't question my orders in combat again," Chris says quietly. "You're dismissed."

It's not insulting. Just a reminder of who's in charge.

Alexander stalks away, the vein in the center of his forehead bulging, his face a dark shade of red. Almost purple. The entire militia has their eyes on Alexander as he shoves his way through the crowd, swearing under his breath. Yet he doesn't continue to argue with Chris, and that alone is the deciding factor in this mini-mutiny moment. Chris calmly unfolds his arms and takes a look around the camp. People disperse, whispering under their breath. I meet Chris's gaze.

"You handled that well," I comment, forcing a smile.

He nods.

Mrs. Young pushes her way through the crowd, reaching for Chris. It's one of those rare moments when her long gray hair is hanging loose to her shoulders, framing her petite face.

"Chris," she says, embracing her son. "You're safe. Thank God."

Chris doesn't reply.

He just returns the hug.

"I'm glad you're safe, too, Cassie," Mrs. Young adds, taking my hand.

Jeff sighs from the corner of the tent. He says, "Did I miss all the action?"

"Nothing like death and blood to put some pep in your step," I reply.

He rolls his eyes.

Whatever. He'll see what it's like soon enough.

"What was Alexander upset about?" I ask, crossing my arms. "I mean, I could be wrong here, but that wasn't a typical victory celebration. He was ticked."

The militiamen are unloading the commandeered trucks. Everything from water bottles to boxes of canned goods have been confiscated from the labor camp – plus, we've got nearly fifty hungry new recruits if the liberated prisoners decide to join us and fight.

"Alexander has a different style than I do," Chris says, taking a seat on a camping chair. He pulls his hair loose from his ponytail, letting his long hair frame his face. "It's not entirely his fault – I was trained the same way, but the difference between us is that I'm looking at our group as a rescue unit rather than a kill squad."

I state squeeze next to him on the chair. "Explain, please?"

Chris sighs.

"In the military, they train you to defend your brothers and kill your enemies," he answers, keeping an eye on the pickups.

"They train you in such a way that you've already mentally accepted the fact that there *will* be casualties on your side. Losses are accepted and acknowledged ahead of time. That's the price of war."

Sophia worms her way through the crowd, walking towards us. She gives me a nod to let me know she made it back to camp safely, and wanders off into the crowd, giving us our privacy.

"As a SEAL, I was trained to kill," he replies. "We specialize in counterterrorism, special reconnaissance, guerilla warfare, even. But we go into that situation knowing that somebody in our group may die – even though we're doing everything we can to prevent that." He pulls my hair away from my face, examining the bruise on my forehead. "What happened to your forehead?"

I touch my temple, feeling soreness there.

"Oh. I'm fine. Go on."

"You need to be checked out by the medic." He stands up, keeping a firm grip around my arm. "Come on."

He starts leading me through the camp.

"You'd make a stellar nurse."

"Thanks."

"So what's the deal with Alexander, then?"

"I had to change my mindset when I started training this militia," Chris explains. "I had to realize that we've got extremely limited numbers in comparison to Omega, and losing any personnel could be devastating. Everybody from old women to little boys is contributing to this war effort, and we can't afford to have anybody killed.

"As a rescue unit, we don't go in solely to kill – although that comes with the mission. This is a war. But we're there to liberate prisoners, take supplies and create chaos. We want to keep everybody on our side alive. That means no blunt maneuvers or strategies that start with the basis of acceptable losses. There *are* no acceptable losses. I want everybody out alive."

We find the medic's tent, and there's a crowd of militiamen gathered around. The people with the most serious wounds have first priority. It could be a while before I'm seen. Chris and I hang back from the tent.

"Alexander's style is upfront and exactly how we'd do it in the military," Chris sighs. "There's nothing wrong with his execution. He's a good soldier. He just doesn't have the right mindset. He can't sacrifice our men like that. It was unnecessary. The goal is to leave with minimal losses. Alexander is going to have to wrap his head around that."

"So long story short, Alexander's just more reckless than you are," I remark.

"No. He sees us as a professional army," he says. "And we're not...yet."

"We will be. I thought we did pretty good tonight."

"We did. There's a lot of room for improvement." He looks me over. "You did well. I'm proud of you."

"Thanks." I twirl my hair around my finger. "So what's next for us?"

Chris cocks an eyebrow.

"Ready for another mission already?"

"Not right this second...but yeah. I know what it's like to be imprisoned, and I'd like to liberate some more POWs. Create some chaos. You know. The basics." I stand on my tiptoes and kiss his cheek. "Thanks for looking out for me."

He hooks his arm around my waist.

"My pleasure."

The rest of the night is spent waiting to be checked out by the combat medics, which are actually a couple of former EMTs who were liberated from Kamaneva's labor camp. By the time I stumble back to my tent with the Young family, the adrenaline has finally worn off and I'm exhausted. I fall asleep on my camping mattress with my clothes on. Later, I'm briefly aware of Chris lying next to me, pulling me into his warmth.

I sleep like a rock until I feel something tugging at my hair.

I slap it away and roll to the side, coming face to face with Isabel's blue eyes.

"Wake up," she grins. "You overslept. Like, a lot."

I sit up and rub the grit out of my eyes.

"What time is it?"

"Who cares? Everybody's eating breakfast already."

I muss my hair with my hands, sniffing my jacket.

Ugh. Smells like smoke.

"Do I look as nasty as I feel?" I ask.

"Worse." Isabel jumps to her feet. "But that's okay. I still like you."

"Thanks."

I stand up and follow her outside. Mrs. Young and some other women in the camp are working on serving breakfast to the army waiting in line to be fed. I stand and stare at the scene. There has never been such a ragtag bunch of fighting men and women in history.

Well…*recent* history, that is.

Chris is already eating at a makeshift table with Derek and Max. He gives me a wave, signaling for me to join them. After I've grabbed some food, I head over, but not before I catch a glimpse of Harry hiding out in the corner of camp again. He's talking to a recruit I've never seen before, and their conversation doesn't last long. A sour expression flashes across Harry's face as he walks away, his eyes briefly flicking to mine. I half expect him to stick his tongue out at me, but instead he levels his gaze and stands, stalking away. No doubt searching for a more suitable dark hole to crawl into and mope.

How inspiring.

"Morning," Chris greets. "Sleep good?"

"Yeah. You?"

"Yes, ma'am."

Derek sizes me up, balancing an empty bowl in his lap.

"Nice work, Hart," he says, giving me a casual salute. "You're a good shot."

"Thanks."

"Yeah, impressive," Max agrees, taking a drink of water. "We would have gotten out of there without too many losses if

Alexander hadn't screwed up at the end and rushed the guards."

"Freaking Alexander Ramos," Derek mutters.

"He won't do it again," Chris says.

They look at him in silence.

"He *won't*. He's set in his ways, but he's not stupid. He's a good soldier." Chris leans forward. "All in all, last night was a very successful mission. Omega's scrambling right now. They have no idea what just hit them."

As I sit and listen to them talk, I get a flashback of myself crouched on the floor of the empty storage facility at Kamaneva's labor camp. I was waiting to be executed. I was going to *die*. I shouldn't be thinking about this right now, but I can't help it. Near death experiences have a way of sticking with you.

I etched my name into that wall.

That little building will never forget me.

Will people remember who we are a hundred years from now? How will this war end? Will we win? Will we lose? Will they even have a name for us in the history books...or will we be a depressing footnote in a teacher's notebook?

"We need a motto," I say suddenly.

"Excuse me?" Derek asks.

"You know. In the movies guerilla warfighters always have a can of spray paint that they use to write their names over all the stuff they've destroyed or conquered from their enemies." I gaze up at the trees, thinking. "We need to leave something behind for Omega to find. Something that tells them *exactly* who they're dealing with. Something that people can remember us by."

"She's right," Chris agrees, his lips curving into a smile. "Half the battle is creating an image. Psychological warfare. Omega will learn to be afraid of us."

"So what's it going to be?" Derek asks.

"I thought we were the Free Army," Max shrugs.

"We are." I take a bite of my food. "We need something short but dangerous. Something easy for Omega to say, you know? Something powerful."

"How about the *tigers*?" Sophia suggests, plopping down beside me. "That was the mascot for the basketball team at the school where Kamaneva set up the labor camp."

"Well...that's good, but not quite," I reply. "We're not tigers. We're..." I close my eyes. "We're like Minute Men or something."

"How about *The Resistance*?" Derek says.

"Almost."

I don't know yet. I'll have to give this some serious thought. If Omega's going to be seeing a lot more of us, they need a name that they'll know and recognize instantly. Something that will *scare* them. Something that they'll be forced to respect. The *Free Army* is good, but...we need something else.

As the day passes, Chris gathers the militia together and gives us a recap of what went down last night, also known as a mission debrief. He congratulates us all on a job well done and tells us what we could have done *better*. He talks about how Alexander rushed the guards at the end, and how we need to avoid sacrificing unnecessary lives if we can avoid it. He talks about improving our aim and making sure we don't break cover too soon.

"We need more ammunition and clothing for the fifty new recruits we picked up last night," he says. "This can be our next opportunity to strike Omega and get the supplies we need at the same time. If we can keep our troops fed and clothed, there's no reason we can't be a serious threat to Omega's forces."

Those of us who have been trained by Chris and his team are supposed to help the newbies that we liberated from the labor camp last night. We are to teach them the basics of fighting.

That means *I* get to teach other people how to shoot.

Oh, yes. The hunted really *have* becomes the hunters.

It will be a few weeks before the new recruits are ready to go out and fight, but we don't want the sting of our attack to be forgotten by Omega. We need to hit them again.

"Omega regularly sends patrols into this area here," Chris says one day, indicating an area on a map being held up by a couple of militiamen. "On the east side of Dunlap, about thirty-eight miles out of Fresno – nearly ten miles from where we are right now. Those patrols are well armed. We could use more weapons and ammo. I say we hit the patrol."

"I say we do, too," Max agrees, folding up the map.

"Me too," I agree.

"I'm coming too," Jeff says, looking like his brother as he stands up, hands balled into fists. "I'm not staying behind this time."

Chris doesn't answer. In truth, Jeff should be out on the front lines with all of us. He knows how to handle a weapon. He's eighteen years old, strong, healthy and willing to fight. I just know better than anybody else that Chris would never forgive himself if something happened to his little brother. But Chris isn't stupid, either. We need every able-bodied men and woman on the front lines, fighting this war. Jeff is more than capable.

Chris nods. "We'll talk," he says quietly.

I know how Chris feels about keeping his family out of the firing line. I don't blame him. I don't want anybody in the Young family to get hurt, either. They're all I have. My dad is missing – who knows if I'll ever see him again? I'd like to hang on to whatever I've got left.

And so would Chris.

I do a lot of sneaking around.

It's cool and dark right now. The moon is shrouded by drifting clouds. We've left the pickups and trucks five miles away. I'm following Chris through tall grass, and we're nearing the main highway. A lump forms in my throat. Dunlap is more wide open than I was expecting.

Max has gone on ahead of us with his team – as usual – setting up the homemade reconnaissance and explosives.

Omega will be passing through in a small convoy, and we intend to ambush them.

It will confuse them and give us time to enter the area, take their weapons and split. We sink into the tall grass, right at the edge of the road, watching the stretch of highway. We're wearing scarves over our faces, covering everything but our eyes. My hair color is also hidden with another scarf, over which I'm wearing a hat.

Keeping our identities secret from Omega will go a long way in keeping us alive. If they know us by sight and by name, they can track us down quicker. So we've found ways to work around that. Every time we bring in new recruits, they're not told anyone's real names. Codenames work. Omega doesn't need to know anything about us – we should be a dangerous mystery to them.

Chris is *Alpha One.*

Thanks to my reputation as a speedy riflewoman, I've been codenamed *Yankee*, if that makes any sense.

Sophia is *Echo.*

We don't refer to each other by our real names unless we're in private, and those who know what our real names are may never use them unless it's absolutely necessary.

"Let's make this clean and fast," Chris says.

"Roger that, *Alpha One.*"

He rolls his eyes.

"What? It's fun to say." I settle back into the prone position, sweeping the road for any signs of Omega. "Right, *Echo*?"

Sophia stifles a laugh beside me.

"Copy that, *Yankee*."

"Shut up, you two," Derek hisses, but I can tell by the way his eyes are crinkling that he's smiling. "They should be coming any minute now."

Heck yeah. Max and his team are making their way back to us, coming around behind our group.

"All set?" Chris whispers.

"Ready to go." Max dips his head. "We'll have to move fast. Some of our scouts are saying there's at least five vehicles. Big ones."

"We can handle that." Chris throws a glance at me. "Stay in place, *Yankee*."

"Yes sir, *Alpha One*."

The clouds momentarily part, letting the moonlight shine through. A shadow falls across my face. I look up, startled, and then relax again when I hear the soft call of an owl. He drifts across the sky and makes an epic dive towards the ground, nabbing a small rodent.

"That's so nasty," Sophia mutters.

"That's the great circle of life," I say.

"Still. Nasty."

"Not if you're an owl."

"Hold. Here they come," Chris snaps.

Because it's so still, I can feel the slight rumble of vehicle engines as they make their way up the road. I look down my rifle sights, shutting my mouth, flicking the safety off. Listening and watching.

Below us, Alexander Ramos is in place with his team. He'll be the first one to hit Omega after the explosion takes out their cars. Despite the arguments and tension between him and Chris, there's no denying that Alexander is a good soldier, and failing to utilize his skills would be a waste of talent.

He just has to learn to be a guerilla fighter.

The trucks come into view. They've got their headlights on, rolling slowly, seemingly unconcerned with hiding themselves from potential enemies. I'm guessing they've never encountered any trouble in this area before. As they round the bend in the road, I brace myself for the explosion. Max is counting down under his breath.

Nothing.

"Where are those detonations?" Chris hisses.

"I don't know." Max leans forward, watching the convoy rumble past the spot in the road where the explosions were supposed to go off. "They didn't go off."

"You've *got* to be kidding me," Sophia says.

As the seconds tick by, the convoy crawls towards us, getting closer to our ambush point. We remain still, camouflaged. "What do we do?" I whisper, tense.

"We can't engage them now," Chris replies. "We can't-"

The sonic thunder of automatic weapons fire cuts him off. Of the five vehicles in the convoy, the first two swerves off the roadway, rubber squealing against the asphalt as the drivers desperately try to control the vehicles. One hits a tree and bursts into flames, spitting billows of black smoke. Another vehicle tumbles down an embankment, doing a rollover, its tires still spinning as it lands on its roof. I stare openmouthed at the sudden destruction and confusion. A daisy chain of linked blasts detonates under the wheels of the remaining vehicles, tossing one aside and forcing the others to grind to a halt.

"What just happened?" Sophia demands.

"I have no idea."

"Engage," Chris says. "Now."

Our team opens fire. I relax into position and set my sights on the scene below. Omega troopers stumble out of their vehicles. Most of them are slow and disoriented, making them easy targets to take down. Rapid gunfire rips through the trees – both from us and from below. Alexander and his team have opened fire, too. Omega troopers are dropping left and right, smoke is spilling into the night sky. Screaming and yelling echoes off the otherwise silent foothills. Omega doesn't even have time to return fire. We're cutting them down too fast. And in the middle of all of this insanity, I'm firing as fast as I can, dropping an empty magazine onto the ground, inserting another one into my gun.

I'm a real Amazon warrior princess these days. Whoopee.

It doesn't take more than a few minutes for the bloodshed to cease – but it seems like hours. My ears are ringing from the gunfire and I'm choking on diesel fumes and smoke.

"Should we go down there?" I ask.

"Let Alexander check it out first," Chris answers.

We stay in position as Alexander brings his team to the so-called "kill zone." They check the dead and attend to the wounded. He gives us the all-clear signal and we slip out of our hiding places and make our way down the side of the hill, walking onto the road, keeping our formation, constantly scanning the perimeter.

"Okay, just like you practiced," Chris tells me.

I kneel at the feet of a dead Omega trooper. I have to make a monumental effort not to gag as I touch his lifeless fingers. They're still warm, reminding me that just a second ago, this guy's heart was beating.

Stop, I warn myself. *Just do your job.*

I take his weapons – guns, ammunition, and knives. The works. Next I strip off his jacket and boots, including the helmet on his head. I also commandeer his socks, because mine are full of holes.

"Pants too," Chris says. "You'll need them, believe me."

Awkward. I shouldn't have to be yanking the pants off dead people, but I guess that's one of the less glamorous aspects of guerilla war fighting. When I'm done, I've got the full uniform of an Omega soldier in my arms, along with all of his gear. Sophia hands me an empty backpack and I stuff the items inside – everything except the rifle. I sling that across my back and toss the backpack to one of the men.

We move fast, collecting everything in record time. When we're done, I have to fight the urge to take a can of spray paint and etch an epic slogan over the vehicles.

"You're thinking of graffiti right now," Sophia remarks.

"You know me too well."

Chris gives the signal and we clear out of the area, retreating into the hills. Our trucks are only parked about a mile from here. Alexander has some of his men take the Omega trucks that are still running. They're full of food, water, and best of all, more weapons. I give him a suspicious look. Obviously *he* was responsible for stopping the convoy when Max's detonations failed.

Max takes his team down the road and checks the explosives he set up. He comes back to us. "Somebody messed with my detonations," he growls. "They were armed and set."

"Nobody knows how to do that," Alexander replies.

"Somebody obviously does."

We cast anxious glances at each other. Is there a traitor in our midst? Or was there simply a technical glitch with Max's explosives? At any rate, Alexander has turned out to be the hero of the day.

"You improvised," Chris states, looking at him. "Nice work."

Alexander shrugs, gruffly moving aside.

"So you set off those explosions, then?" I ask.

Alexander nods.

"Never hurts to be prepared."

Huh. Chris was right. Alexander *is* a good soldier.

Weird, but good.

Two of the Omega trucks are still drivable, but the rest of us will have to go on foot to the rally point. Alexander's team takes the trucks, and we're left behind to experience all the joys of a hike in the foothills.

"Let's cut cross country through the mountain pass," Max says. "It'll be faster."

Chris nods. We follow the curve of the highway and hike uphill onto a dirt road, passing a couple of impressive rock formations. An iron fence has been smashed open and twisted. We jump over it and continue through the road, the bushes and trees eerie against the dark, cloudy sky.

"I hope you know where you're going," Sophia tells Max.

"Of course I do." He points. "This is easier than climbing over the big hill. This just cuts right through it to the other side."

"Right, right."

As we wind our way deeper into the side of the hill, I notice small buildings.

"What's all this?" I wonder.

"I don't know," Chris replies. "Keep your eyes open."

We keep to our patrol formations, just like we practiced. Chris sends a scout to check out the area ahead, while Sophia and I bring up the rear of the group. We're always watching. Always listening. Always alert.

If there's one thing that's just as dangerous as Omega, it's nomads and vandals. They hide in abandoned compounds or houses, living off the leftover food of the previous occupants. Based on my previous experience with desperate people wandering around the state, I've come to the conclusion that it's better to avoid them if you can.

The buildings are spaced far apart in some places, and in other areas they're close together. Chain link fences are nestled into the side of the hills. Trails weave between those fences. Trees and bushes are growing around the perimeter, and there are thick cables surrounding each chain link fence. They look like barriers.

"This is creepy," Sophia says under her breath.

I have to agree.

"Let's check it out," somebody suggests.

"No. We need to get out of the area. Omega will be sending in backup to look for that missing convoy," Chris replies.

"Hey, look!" I spot a small, brown wooden directory on the edge of the road. I head towards it, flipping out my commandeered Omega flashlight. I flick it on.

Project Survival's Cat Haven

Beneath is a map of the entire compound; tiger cages, leopard cages, even a lion enclosure. Sophia is staring at it with wide eyes. "You don't think any of those things are still here, do you?" she asks.

Chris raises an eyebrow.

"If they got out of their cages, it's possible," he answers. "Otherwise they're probably dead if this place was evacuated after the EMP."

I turn off the flashlight, my heart racing in my chest.

All I need is to come face to face with a starving panther to make this night even more exciting. I mean, come *on*. Chris squeezes my hand, sensing my unease, and we walk away from the directory board.

"Maybe we should go around after all," Max says. "Just in case."

"What? Afraid of the little kitty cats?" Chris quips.

"*Little*?" I roll my eyes. "They're *jungle* cats, Chris."

He tugs on my arm, his signal for me to keep my mouth shut. I zip my lips and keep a tight grip on my rifle. Personally, I'd rather be holding Chris's hand right now, but I'm a soldier these days...and how would that look? By the time we reach the other side of the mountain, I'm afraid to take a deep breath because of the noise it will make. Then again, if we *are* being hunted by a wild cat, there's not a lot I can do about it.

"That was mildly terrifying," I comment.

"Not too bad, actually," Chris grins. "I'd say me and a big cat are evenly matched, wouldn't you?"

"I don't think that question is worth an answer."

We reach the trucks shortly. We throw our stuff into the back and drive into the night, retracing our path back to base. Everyone's waiting for us when we return, including Derek's team. He stayed behind to guard the camp and keep everybody in line while we were gone. With our militia getting bigger and bigger, more people have to be left behind to keep law and order around here.

Sophia and I take our stuff back to our tent and start messing around with it. I rip the Omega patch off the sleeve of the uniform from the dead trooper and replace it with a blue armband. I look over the gun and ammunition, checking our supplies. Even though we got our hands on a lot of stuff, it won't be enough to last for long. The militia is growing every day. We need more weapons, more ammo, more food, more water and of course, more space.

All of these people bring lots of extra noise, so Chris is thinking about moving our basecamp farther into the mountains. There are pros and cons to that idea. On the plus side, we'll have more freedom to practice training and indulge in little things like campfires because there won't be as much of a chance that we'll be spotted by enemies. On the negative side, we'll be farther away from Omega hotspots, therefore conducting raids and ambushes will be a longer process because we'll have to travel farther. Long-range patrols could keep us in the loop about Omega activities while the rest of our forces pull back deeper into the mountains.

In the end, I think safety will win over distance. But there's always the option of breaking down our forces into smaller camps. I'm not too crazy about that idea, though. I'd prefer to keep our militia together.

"Do you think we're doing the right thing?" Sophia asks me, picking at her commandeered uniform.

"What do you mean?"

"We're actually killing people, Cassidy," she replies, looking up. Her lower lip is trembling. "Are we doing the right thing?"

I fold my hands in the center of my lap.

"It's kill or be killed. Nothing's like it used to be," I say slowly. "It's not like we have a choice."

"But why are *we* doing it?"

"Who else is going to? It's our *duty* to protect our home." I sigh. "It's just the way things are. If we don't fight back, Omega will kill us all. Especially now that we've been attacking them. We're playing offense *and* defense. They've been murdering and enslaving people left and right. Either we put up a fight or we let them eat us alive. It's that simple."

Sophia takes a deep breath.

"But what if this is all for nothing?" she says. "What if we do all of this fighting and sacrificing and Omega still wins? Because if they're really a huge army with help from places like Russia or China or whatever, we're kind of screwed, aren't we? When we were at the labor camp, they were having us harvest food for something *big*. You said they were getting ready to bring in more troops." She looks me straight in the eye. "And then Mrs. Young said the big cities have been attacked with chemical weapons, and the rumors about a nuclear bomb on the east coast may or may not be true. How do we stand a chance against an army with that kind of power?"

I run my hands through my hair.

"We're motivated."

"And they're *not*?"

"We actually have something worth fighting for."

"What?"

"Freedom."

She makes a face.

"How many people have said that," she says, "and then died?"

"Millions." I stand up, dusting the dirt off my pants. "I can't think of anything I'd rather die for, though. I'd rather die fighting than hiding in a hole somewhere. Or enslaved."

Sophia slowly nods.

"I guess so."

"You *guess* so?" I hold out my arms. "Sophia, look around you! We were *enslaved* together, remember? Kamaneva almost executed me on the sidewalk of an elementary school. That's not *normal*, is it? We're fighting for normalcy. We're fighting for what we lost. I think that's a worthy cause, don't you?"

She rises to her feet, and when she speaks, her voice wobbles. "It *is* worthy," she whispers. "You're right. I just...sometimes I think I can't do this another day."

"We all feel like that." I wrap my arms around her neck and pull her into a hug. "Nobody said fighting a war was going to be easy."

"Your boyfriend makes it look like a walk in the park."

"He does not," I laugh. "He just knows how to inspire people."

We turn to watch him. He's standing on the other side of the camp. His muscular arms are folded across his chest, his hair pulled into a tight ponytail. He's listening intently to what one of the soldiers is saying. After a few beats of silence, he responds, pats him on the back, and moves on to the next person waiting to speak with him.

"He's becoming quite a leader," Sophia remarks.

I feel myself smiling.

"Yeah, he is."

The truth is, we've all changed. We've all matured. We've all seen things that have forced us to grow up. It will bring out the best in some of us. In others, it will bring out the worst.

But when it comes right down to it, at the end of the day, we're all on the same team.

We're all fighting to get our freedom back.

And that's when the name hits me.

Freedom Fighters.

Chapter Twelve

If anyone would have told me seven months ago that I would be spending my college years as a guerilla warfighter with freaking Rambo as my boyfriend, I would have said they were crazy. But life is weird like that. And considering the fact that everybody's lives have been turned inside out by the effects of the EMP and the invasion of America, everything's been on a whole different level of weird.

Weird on steroids.

It's July now, and the heat is brutal. There have been days when the hundred-degree weather is torture. It's hard to keep cool. The only thing we can do is stay in the shelter of the trees during the day and move around at night. We've been consistently hitting Omega where it hurts: convoys, supply depots, anything and everything that will effect their ability to feed their troops or keep their morale up. This is not just a game of firepower. It's a game of mind over matter.

Which one of us is more motivated to win?

We've relocated our camp to a higher elevation. It's easier to keep hidden when we're farther away from the valley, anyway. And since Omega is constantly combing through the area searching for our "headquarters," we constantly change the location of our camp, too. If we stay in one place for too long, we'll be found.

The Free Army – or the *Freedom Fighters*, as we've come to be called – have become pretty well known in the area. Our forces have expanded. We've got a few hundred people in our ranks now, and Chris is becoming an impressive leader. He's logical, fair and knowledgeable. People trust him.

I've become something different, too. Instead of just running with the pack, I work with Derek, Max, Alexander and Chris to train the new recruits. I've got responsibilities. I've got people who look to me for advice.

I never thought I'd see *that* day.

Despite the fact that our army is made up completely of volunteers – most of which are civilians who have never been in a fight in their lives – we're well organized. Chris goes to a lot of trouble to train the new recruits, and to keep the older ones' skills sharpened. Ever since the day Chris almost killed Harry Lydell, I've been painfully aware of the fact that all it takes is one wrong move to turn organization into murder. It's easy to think that all you have to do is get a bunch of people together and fight the bad guys, but it's not that simple.

It requires structure.

Chris is the head honcho in this camp, something along the lines of a mini-general, but he makes few decisions without consulting his officers first, which would be Derek, Max and Alexander, who are all platoon leaders. They each command a force of about thirty to fifty fighting men and women. I'm not in charge of a platoon, but I *am* in charge of training the new recruits. Yes, the "newbies" are all mine. I teach them the basics, go with them on missions and make sure everybody is doing their job. We work as a team, so we basically go on a majority vote. Everyone has a say in the activities that go on at the basecamp.

But sometimes things aren't so easy.

When an organization gets big, there will inevitably be people who will betray you. In this war, betrayal can lead to the death of everybody in the militia, so it has to be dealt with swiftly and effectively. In the event that somebody commits a horrible crime, the officers convene with Chris. All it takes is three command level officers to vote for a punishment to make it happen. So far we've been lucky. We've only had to punish people for petty crimes like stealing extra food rations, hoarding ammunition and getting into fights. But at some point, someone will do something so big that we'll have to figure out how to handle the situation.

Maybe we should just build a jail.

At any rate, we're not the only guerilla war fighters in the area. Other militia groups have been popping up in the state, an encouraging piece of information we learned from the Underground, a network of rebel militiamen who carry messages up and down the state for people like us. Like undercover pony express riders, they travel on foot from one destination to the next, passing on messages to fellow rebels. They have a dangerous job. They travel alone, they travel fast, and they travel light. The cover of darkness is their best friend as they run from camp to camp, sending messages between the rebel "communities." If they're caught, they'll either be killed or tortured to death.

So of course their number one priority is to avoid getting caught.

Everything has gotten faster, cleaner and more efficient. The Freedom Fighters are turning into a well-oiled resistance front, and I'm starting to find my groove. I never thought I'd fit into a society like this, but life has a way of surprising you. For the first time in my life, I actually feel like I belong somewhere. Whether that's a good thing or a bad thing, I haven't decided yet.

"I have some new information for you, Cassie," Chris says one day. The scorching July heat is all but singeing my eyebrows off, so I'm huddled under the shade of a tall tree. The camp is busy with activity – there is no such thing as an idle moment here. Even our sleeping hours have purpose.

"Cassie?"

I blink and look up, yawning.

"Sorry. I was dozing."

He smiles and sits beside me, one of the few moments lately when he's been relaxed enough to do this. As the weeks have passed, the stress and pressure of being in charge of this militia have changed him. He's even more logical and methodical than he used to be. He's a lot busier, too. People depend on him to make life-changing decisions. It must be difficult to carry a burden like that.

"What's up?" I say.

"Underground gave us some new information," he replies.

I lean forward. "Is it good or bad news?"

"Both. The good news is, there's a rebel militia force called the *Mountain Rangers* headed our way."

I nod. We've all heard of the *Rangers*. They're second only to the *Freedom Fighters* in notoriety.

"What's the bad news?" I ask.

"The bad news is, we have to decide if we want to join forces with the *Rangers* or if we want to keep our group separate. Joint operations change the dynamics. Right now our men work really well together. Bringing in an ally could either mess things up or make us stronger."

"We don't know enough about the Rangers to make a judgment, do we?"

"The *Rangers* are, as far as we know, very similar to our militia. They use guerilla war fighting tactics, they're quick, they're hearty and they're no friends to Omega."

That makes them on our side, I guess. But Chris is right. Exposing ourselves to anybody is a monumental risk.

"Why don't you meet with their commander and talk to him about it?" I suggest. "Just you and him. Don't drag everybody else into it until you're absolutely sure that we need their help."

"We don't really *need* anybody's help," Chris replies. "But we could do a lot *more* with an extra force." He stares at something in the distance, thinking. "That's not a bad idea, Cassie. I should do that."

"Can you get a message through to the *Rangers* using the Underground?"

"I should be able to."

"Who's in charge of their group?"

"I don't know. Everyone's got codenames."

"Right. *Alpha One.*" I grin. "What's their leader's codename?"

"We'll find out." He stretches his long legs across the dirt, studying my hand, tracing it with his finger. "The Underground *also* mentioned a huge Omega supply depot being stocked on the outskirts of the foothills. A lot of food and water are going in there. Omega's tightening up security around the place – it's important."

"So we need to hit it, then?" I ask.

"Essentially."

"Do we have enough manpower for that?"

"I think so. We're outnumbered, but we're smarter. And faster." Chris looks down at our hands. "How are you holding up?"

It's a sudden question.

And something he hasn't asked me in a while.

"I'm fine," I say.

"That's not very descriptive."

"I *am*." I bite back a smile. "I miss you, though. Even though I'm around you all the time, it's like you're not really here. You're always so busy."

Chris presses the palm of his hand against my cheek.

"I'm sorry," he says. "But you understand, right?"

"Understand that people need you?" I dip my head. "Yeah. I do. I just miss you, that's all."

"I know." He kisses my forehead. "You've adapted extremely well. You're a good soldier. I'm not the only one people are looking up to, you know."

"I know. That's what scares me."

"What? Respect?"

I gaze up at him.

"I guess so. When people respect you, they *expect* a lot from you. There's so much responsibility. People's lives are at stake." I sigh. "I don't feel up to being a hardcore rebel leader all the time."

Chris takes both of my hands in his.

"That's why people like you. You're human, but you try to do the right thing no matter what the situation is." His eyes flick to the edge of camp, where the women are doing their daily food preparation. "Always try to do the right thing. Go with your gut instinct."

"I'm not a leader like you are."

"Yes, you are. Just in a different way." His expression softens. "You give good advice, too. I'll see if I can get in contact with the *Rangers'* leader. It might be helpful if we combine forces at some point. But until then, we need to get ready to hit that supply depot."

"How far away is it?"

"About twenty miles. It's out of the foothills. On the edge of the valley outside a little town called Sanger." He looks at me. "Are you up for that?"

I roll my eyes. Leaving the safety of the hills is a major risk.

"Why wouldn't I be?"

"Just thought I'd ask," he chuckles, standing up. "We should hit it soon, before they get a chance to set everything up completely. They'll be beefing up security anyway because of what we've been doing in the area, plus it will be crawling with Omega patrols."

I agree. Ever since the Freedom Fighters have started fighting back against Omega, more militia groups have formed. All people needed to see was one group taking the initiative and hitting back at the enemy. Omega's got an entire state full of rebels and guerilla fighters on their hands these days. It can't be easy being an invading army. Not with people like us around.

But what we haven't talked about much is the fact that Omega is gearing up to receive backup. Sophia and I figured that out a long time ago when we were imprisoned in the labor camp. It's obvious they're going to need more manpower if they're going to kill off the rebels completely. Chris knows this. I know this. Most of the people in this militia know it. The question is, what will we do when Omega's backup *does* arrive? What kind of backup is it going to be? Where will it come from?

Can we survive it?

The *Mountain Rangers* are hard to contact.

Just like our militia, everything is kept anonymous and secret, because let's face it: you can't trust anybody these days. Of course, I didn't trust anybody before the EMP, either. But that was just me. Now everybody has come down to my level.

Ironic.

The Underground is an efficient but slow means of communication, and it will take a few days to find out if they want to have a pow-wow with Chris about joining forces. Until then, our focus is the supply depot that Omega is setting up. It's located on the edge of Sanger, about twenty or so miles away from Squaw Valley. Because we've moved our campsite farther into the hills, it will be a little bit more of a journey for us to reach the depot in our trucks. It will also be hard to be stealthy, because once we leave the shelter of the hills, we'll be out in the open. Wide grassy plains aren't that great for our style of fighting, but Chris will find a way to make it work.

The best thing we can do is take away Omega's food, water, fuel and ammunition. What Chris likes to call the "meat and potatoes" of war. Because that's the one thing that everybody needs to stay alive. That's why hitting supply depots are so important. And we're getting better and better at it.

My dad would be proud.

And shocked. I don't know if he ever expected me to amount to anything. I mean, sure, I'd planned on getting a degree in criminal justice before the EMP hit and the world went down the drain, but at the time I had no way to attain that goal. No money, no job, no friends, no family. I was a speck of nothing in a big world that was passing me by.

Now I have a purpose, at least.

As we gear up for the journey down the mountain to hit the Omega base in the nearby valley city of Sanger, my nerves are all over the place. I give an Oscar-winning performance of calmness for Chris and the rest of the camp, but on the inside,

I'm being eaten alive with anxiety. We've never tried to attack a target this big before, and we've really never tried to hit anything outside of the foothills.

Something about this whole mission seems...*off.*

Go with your gut instinct, Chris told me. But my gut instincts aren't like his. Mine are tainted with fear and raw nerves, which makes the "instinct" a little hard to decipher. How do you know what's real and what's not?

I'm guessing this is why I'm not in charge.

The night we're supposed to carry out our mission on the supply depot finally rolls in. Chris is wound tight – more so than usual. My stomach is tied into knots. Even Alexander seems tense about the situation. I guess it's natural. We *are* wandering out of our comfort zone.

"Maybe we should just wait and see if the Rangers will help us," I suggest to Chris. We're waiting by our pickup truck, checking our gear. "This is a big target. We've got a lot of men, but backup could never hurt, right?"

"We don't have time to wait around for the Underground to bring us a message back from the *Rangers,*" Chris replies, tugging on his jacket collar. "I want to hit the depot before they've got everything completely mobilized. Before they get everything set up. We *can't* wait."

I sigh.

"I just have a bad feeling about this one, Chris."

He presses his lips together, meeting my gaze.

"Don't let fear back you into a corner," he warns. "This is new for us, so it's intimidating. But we're more than capable. You know that."

"I know. But-"

"-No. Cassie, remember what I said about people respecting you? You're an example. Don't let people see you being afraid. Be brave. Even if you don't feel that way."

I blink back tears.

"Yes, sir."

He traces my cheek with the back of his hand.

"We'll be fine."

How many times are we going to have to go through this kind of scene? I guess that's what war does to you. It's repetitive. It's also terrifying. Going to college and getting my criminal justice degree would have been a lot easier than this.

Leave it to me to do things the hard way.

"Be careful," Isabel says.

She's wrapped up in an oversized windbreaker. Her wild blonde hair is sticking up in every direction, and her baby blue eyes are tinged with red. She's as tired as the rest of us, despite the fact that she doesn't do any fighting. Living in an active warzone is enough.

"We will be." I give her a hug. "Take care of everything until we get back."

"How long will you be gone?"

"We should be back by morning."

Chris musses her hair.

"See you, kid." He gives her a smile and walks to the center of the camp. It's time to run through the plan one more time before we move out. I walk around the edge of the ring, spotting Harry in the crowd. He's talking animatedly to somebody, but he's too far away for me to make out what he's saying. I inch closer, straining to hear. Chris steps into the middle of the circle and starts speaking.

"This will be the biggest target we've hit to date," he says. "Let's go through the plan one more time and make sure everybody's completely clear on what they're supposed to do..."

The man that Harry's talking to has his back turned to me, and I can't see who it is in the darkness. I weave through the crowd, trying to concentrate on Chris's speech and Harry's movements at the same time.

"...You just watch yourself," I hear.

Harry's gaze snaps to the left. He sees me. He stiffens and mutters something under his breath. The man he's talking to turns around, glaring at me. Alexander Ramos. I suck in my breath. Harry takes a few steps backwards and melts into the crowd, throwing a nervous glance over his shoulder.

"Well?" Alexander demands.

I open and close my mouth a few times, unsure of what to say.

He scowls and brushes past me.

"Watch yourself, Hart."

His tone is harsh. Harry and Alexander disappear into the crowd in two different directions. My mind is spinning. What could those two possibly be talking about?

I move back through the audience to catch the tail end of Chris's talk.

"It's the same principle as all of the attacks we've done before," he's saying, "only on a larger scale. We'll still surround the depot on four sides, and Max and his team will still open the gates for us...but this depot isn't fully operational yet, so I'm counting on security being a little more lax than what we've experienced in the past. Does anybody have any questions?"

Silence.

"Good. Remember, in the event that something *does* go wrong," he continues, "We revert to using our backup plan." A smile touches his lips, and I instantly know what he's talking about. "Surround the enemy, take cover, and start firing. If they try to break through our lines, just keep retreating and moving with them. Create an inescapable circle of fire. It will be unlike anything Omega's ever been hit with. Any more questions?"

Nope. Chris's father steps forward and offers a brief prayer over the camp. When he's done, I trail behind Chris and corner him back at the truck.

"Alexander Ramos was talking to Harry," I say.

"Yeah?" He looks at his notebook, biting his lower lip.

"You don't find that highly suspicious?"

Chris opens the driver door and gestures for me to crawl inside.

"No. Somebody needs to keep Harry in line."

"No. They were *talking*. Like, engaging in actual chitchat. It wasn't cool."

"Cassie…" Chris literally picks me up and moves me towards the door. "Get in. We're leaving now. If Alexander was talking to Harry, it wasn't because he was plotting world domination. He's a rough guy, but he's not evil."

I slide into the passenger seat and roll the window down.

"I disagree," I shrug. "I think the dude is creepy."

"He's not warm and fuzzy, but he's not a bad guy."

I disagree with that, too. Alexander is very unpredictable, plus he walks around with a chip on his shoulder. He resents Chris for taking away his position of leadership. I can see it in his face every time I look at him.

But what do I know? I'm not in charge.

I'm just going off instinct.

We move out. We've got about a dozen trucks loaded with militiamen. The other trucks have already gone on without us. They'll meet us at a pre-planned rally point down the road. We're traveling separately to keep the engine noise down – plus, it's safer for all involved if we're not traveling in one giant wagon train. A bigger group means a bigger target, and that's not how guerilla war fighters roll.

Sophia jumps into the back of the truck. We lock gazes through the window. She nods, giving me a Girl Scout salute and a weak smile. "It's going to be okay," she mouths.

"I know," I say.

By the time we hit the dusty road, my nerves have calmed. I've gone from raw fear to acceptance of the situation, which is what happens to me before every mission these days. And once the fighting actually starts, adrenaline takes over and I feel like a ninja warrior.

All in all, the drive to Sanger is long. We take our time picking our way through back roads, avoiding the main highway, and only hitting open areas when we absolutely have to. Eventually it becomes impossible to stay away from the wide-open spaces, because let's face it: that's what happens when you leave the mountains. You break cover.

I haven't been out of the foothills in so long that the expanse of open space blows my mind. I feel like an ant under a microscope. Totally exposed. I can tell that the situation is bothering Chris, too. He keeps shifting in his seat and checking the area surrounding us every five seconds.

We reach the rally point at last. It's a grove of trees nestled behind a low hill. It's basically right around the corner from Sanger, and it will give us enough time and space to make it on foot to the objective without drawing attention to ourselves. The last thing we need is to march into town like a circus parade. *That* would be slightly conspicuous.

I climb out of the truck and find Sophia. We give each other a warm hug.

"Be careful," I say.

"You too." She forces a smile. "Dejavu, huh?"

"Yeah."

"The things we do for this country."

"I know. Crazy, right?"

We hug each other one more time before separating into our designated groups. I stay close to Chris's shoulder as we disperse into the tall grass, leaving the cover of the vehicles and the small hill. No one speaks. Any order or command is given through hand signals, but for the most part, we already know the plan. We've raided camps and convoys before. We know how to do this.

This is just...different.

Wide open. Bigger. Exposed.

If you can break out of a labor camp, you can do this, I tell myself.

My hair has grown long enough in the past few months to pull into a tight braid, keeping the strands out of my face. I cinch up my face scarf and check my gear for the thousandth time as we get closer to our target.

As we finally edge around the hill, I spot the depot. It's located on the brink of an empty field. It was probably a packing shed before the EMP went down, and judging by the size of the buildings, I'm guessing it was a big one. The signs have been stripped, and a lot of the equipment has been commandeered by Omega. But there's one thing that sets this apart from the other supply depots I've seen: there's no fence.

The usual chain link fence with the coils of deadly barbed wire are completely missing.

"Something's wrong with this picture," I say.

"This depot isn't fully operational yet, remember?" Derek replies. He's crouched on my right hand side, his blonde hair hidden under a black hat. "They're not expecting to be attacked this far from the mountains. We've never hit anything out of the foothills before."

"No." Chris shakes his head. "They know militia groups are waiting to hit targets like this. They wouldn't leave it unprotected unless there wasn't anything inside."

"It could be a trap," I state.

Derek stares at me.

"What? It *could* be."

I give him a *look*.

We just sit there under the dark sky and stare at the depot. Omega trucks are parked around the building, but there aren't any lights. No signs of life. Something is seriously whacked.

"I don't like this," I whisper. "Chris, what do we do?"

He folds his hands under his chin and studies the depot for a few more minutes before replying. "Derek, detail some scouts. Recon the objective. Report back here."

That's Chris's way of saying, "Check out the depot and see what's up."

He nods.

"Yes, sir."

We wait in tense silence as Derek and a couple of the men creep to the depot and check out the perimeter. They disappear from sight at one point and I find myself holding my breath, hoping I don't hear a sudden scream and a blast of gunfire. It's happened before.

Ten long minutes pass before the scouts come back. I exhale and Chris leans forward, listening. "It's dead down there," Derek breathes. "There's nothing. No lights, no generators, nothing. But there are trucks, and there *have* been Omega troops in the area no more than twenty-four hours ago. It's like they evacuated."

"Why would they do that?" I ask.

"Maybe they heard we were coming," Derek suggests.

"No. Not possible," Chris replies. "They wouldn't evacuate a facility because a militia group was coming to attack, anyway. Besides, why would they leave vehicles behind? They would beef up security because they'd want us dead." He furrows his brow. "If they're gone, there could be valuable supplies left inside."

"We should go check it out."

"I don't want everybody checking it out at once. Too risky." He looks over his shoulder. "Derek, you stay here with your men. I'll take my platoon. Keep your eyes open."

"You got it, sir."

"Let's move out," Chris says.

We proceed into the field, skirting the edges and staying under cover as we approach the depot. The thick silence of the night isn't doing anything to make me feel better about this situation. I look back over my shoulder, but it's impossible to see Derek or the rest of our groups. They're camouflaged too well.

As we get close to the depot, I study the surroundings. Tire tracks crisscross the dirt parking lot. Electrical machinery that was killed by the EMP is piled outside the main building in a large heap. Chris signals a few of the men and they round the edges of the main building, climbing the sides. We wait in the shadows, listening and watching for signs of danger.

One of the men pulls himself up to a window. He takes a quick look around and starts climbing back down to the ground. He jogs towards us along with the other men.

"Well?" Chris asks.

"It's empty."

"*What*?"

"Totally empty. There's nothing in there."

I bite my lip, alarm spiking through me.

"We need to get out of here," I say.

Chris doesn't disagree, but he doesn't say anything either.

"How could they...?" He trails off, lost in his own thoughts. A terrified scream rips through the air at that moment. A woman's scream – one of our own. We instinctively drop to the ground and focus our sights across the field. Something's happening. I hear voices and gunfire and then, I turn my head. Because I'm pressed against the ground, I have a great view of the underside of the Omega trucks parked on the property. My eyes settle on a blinking black package attached to the bottom of the bumper of one of the vehicles.

"Oh, my God," I breathe. "It's a bomb."

Chris snaps his gaze in my direction, realization hitting us at the same time.

"Run!" he yells.

A simple command, but universal. We jump up and book it just as the first bomb detonates. I'm running, so the explosion hits me like a brick wall. I feel the impact slam into my back and send me flying forward several feet. I skid on my stomach and roll over a few times, scraping against dirt and rocks. Metallic tasting blood pools in my mouth. I must have bit my tongue.

I scramble to my feet, only to fall back down again, dizzy and disoriented. My ears are ringing. Chris grabs my arm and helps me find my balance. I look back over my shoulder and gasp. Three or four of the militiamen in our group are lying motionless on the ground about thirty feet behind us. The Omega truck that exploded is nothing more than a hulking mass of smoking, twisted metal. I'm vaguely aware of rapid gunfire in the background, but my ringing ears make it difficult to gauge the distance of the weapons.

Chris drags me into the tall grass and suddenly the entire area is alive with lights and movement. Another Omega vehicle detonates on the edge of the property, sending shockwaves through the field. Luckily, none of our men are close enough to it to be killed, but Max's group is probably more than a little bit singed.

Omega troops swarm out of the wooded areas bordering the fields, either drawing our men out in the open or pushing them back into the hills. Both are bad. I don't even have time to take aim and shoot. All I can do is run.

Because we've walked right into a trap.

I spot Derek's group going head to head with an Omega patrol. Men and women are knocked to the ground. Shot, knifed, kicked, smashed, punched. The end product is always death. The adrenaline rush I've been expecting finally hits me, but it's tainted with horror. All around me our soldiers are being slaughtered. Omega troopers are boxing us in from all sides. They were waiting for us. Watching us as we approached the building.

How could they have known we were coming tonight?

There's a spy in your camp, my gut tells me.

I crawl through the grass, following Chris's lead. We need to reach cover, otherwise we're going to die. Period. We finally get to Derek's group, but the only cover we have here is the tall grass.

These open fields are lethal.

I take out my gun, but I don't even have time to use it. An Omega trooper fires at me from twenty feet away, but I see him moving. I duck out of the way and hit the ground, bringing the gun into my shoulder. Powered with superhuman levels of adrenaline and desperation, I sight him, squeeze the trigger, and take him out. Just like that.

I stay right there on the ground, hidden in the shadows, taking out as many troopers as I can until it's impossible for me to stay in the same place anymore. One of our militiamen accidentally steps on my back, leaving a muddy footprint on the rear panel of my jacket. Yeah. Time to move and stick to maneuvers I know inside and out: Shoot, move and communicate.

Chris is fighting next to Max. Both of them are using every weapon at their disposal, everything from guns to their fists. But Omega keeps coming. They continue to swarm out of the hills like grasshoppers. It's the most terrifying thing I've ever seen – and I've seen some pretty scary stuff since the EMP went down. Sophia literally crashes into me, running at full speed out of the woods. We both tumble to the ground and I look up, my eyes landing on her pursuer, an Omega trooper. I spring to my feet, knock his rifle sideways and kick him hard in the gut. He bends forward, the air rushing out of his lungs. I slam the stock of my rifle across his head and he rolls to the ground, scrambling awkwardly for his weapon. I don't mess around. This is life or death. I take my rifle, squeeze the trigger and land a close range shot to his chest. He's so close to me that I actually feel a spray of hot blood splatter across my cheeks as he falls backwards, dead on the ground.

Sophia grabs my arm.

"I can't find Alexander," she says, covered in sweat. "I think he's hurt."

I meet her gaze.

"Are you serious?"

"Retreat!" Max yells. "Fall back! Rally point One!"

That's just another way of saying, "We're screwed. Run for your lives."

But there's nowhere to retreat. Omega's got us

surrounded. We're closed in on all sides. The militiamen that have been pushed back to the supply depot are being caught in the land mines and IEDs set up by the Omega troopers. A few militiamen find themselves cornered against the warehouse. One sweep of an automatic weapon is all it takes to kill them in less than three seconds.

When I think things can't get any worse, I'm blinded with white light. Sophia and I shield our faces, confused. What the heck is this? A UFO invasion? Are aliens finally taking over the planet?

I wouldn't be surprised.

Please, take it. There's not much left.

My eyes adjust and I focus on the source of the light. Floodlights. Omega is firing up their backup generators and powering floodlights on top of the depot, shooting the beams of light into the fields. Making it easier for them to pick us off. My heart sticks in my throat.

We really *are* dead.

But wait. I spot a familiar figure standing on the edge of the depot. A flash of dark hair. A tall, muscular frame. He's kneeling on the ground. Alexander Ramos. He's watching the proceedings as blood runs down the side of his neck. He's wounded. Badly. I find myself moving towards him, stopping only to look back and make sure Chris and Sophia are still alive. They are, and they're putting up a valiant fight, but a wall of Omega troopers are pushing our militia farther and farther back. There won't be any escape once they reach that point.

I stop and stare at Alexander. He looks at me. We don't say anything. A brief thought flashes through my head: *He's a good soldier. He's just a little rough around the edges.* He looks at me like I'm the most annoying thing on the planet – which is debatable, given the situation – and shakes his head.

"Get *out* of here," he hisses, clutching his shoulder. Blood oozes down his shirt. "Now."

"Let me help you," I stutter, shocked at his appearance.

"Just *keep moving*," he commands, wincing. And then, "Please."

I don't hesitate.

As I'm working my way across the field, I see someone else. Harry Lydell. He's standing motionless next to an Omega vehicle on the other side of the property, a safe distance away from the battlefield. He's unarmed, watching everything with catlike curiosity, and something about that *really* bothers me. I stalk towards him, my weapon raised.

"What are you doing here?" I demand.

"You really are stupid," he says, annunciating slowly. He stares down the barrel of my rifle. "You walked right into this."

"*You*?" I gape at him. "You betrayed us?"

"Cassidy, I was never *with* you in the first place." His eyes shift to the right and then snap back to me. "I've been with Omega since day one."

"But the militia gave you your freedom," I say, shocked. "They saved you from Omega."

"No. Omega gave me my freedom. I've been spying on you since that first day I started working with you in the fields." A twisted smile crawls across his face. "When I was *liberated* by the militia, it made things...difficult. It took a long time to get back in contact with my commander."

"You're really disgusting, you know that?" I spit.

"Oh, I know. Don't flatter me, Cassidy."

"You do realize I'm pointing a gun at your head, right?"

"You won't kill me." He chuckles. "You have trouble killing people you have a relationship with."

"My relationship with you is non-existent. You know what? Maybe I'll save everybody the trouble-"

I never get to finish my sentence, which is sad, because I was just getting to the best part. Something knocks me sideways and I hit the ground with an unattractive thud. A fiery pain explodes just below my ribcage. I look down and press my hand against my side. I lift my hand up, horrified to see my palm dripping in blood.

I've been shot.

I kneel on the ground, too scared for the pain to sink in...yet. Harry stands there and observes me. Like a specimen in a cage. He takes a few steps forward and grabs my rifle before I can even think to react, effectively disarming me. I tilt my head up, clutching my stomach, focusing in on a pair of knee-high leather boots. I follow the boots up to a pair of dark pants, a jacket and a familiar face.

"Kamaneva," I state, trembling.

She doesn't say a word. She only raises an eyebrow, casually holding the gun in her hand that just landed a whopper to my side. There's too much going on around me for the realization of all that's happened to really hit home. I'm frozen. Unmovable.

"Well done, Harry," Kamaneva says, her voice emotionless. "As for you, Cassidy: Nice try."

If I could feel my stomach, I'm sure it would be churning with anxiety right about now. But the bottom half of my body is going numb, and with it, so is my brain. Everything's getting fuzzy. Not even my adrenaline rush is going to keep me awake for long.

Or alive.

Desperation sets in. Kamaneva is trying to kill me...*again*. I slowly move my bloody, sweaty hand towards my belt, leaning forward enough to hide the movement. "They're all as good as dead," Harry says, looking at Kamaneva. "They're completely boxed in."

"You of all people should know that our militia can get out of this," I reply, gritting my teeth. The pain train is pulling into the station. "You've seen us fight before."

"Actually, I haven't. I was always left behind at camp. Nobody trusted me." He flashes a wicked smile. "Rightfully so."

"Traitor."

Yeah. That's the worst insult I can dream up right now. Because Kamaneva's going to blow my brains out in about five seconds and I have to move fast. I close my fingers around the hilt of Jeff's knife hidden in my boot, pull it out of its sheath, and snap it forward, flinging it at Kamaneva's chest. She deftly steps aside and it grazes her arm. It gives me the split second I need to make my move. I jump up and make a mad dash back towards the battlefield. Back towards Chris. I run in a zig-zag pattern, throwing off Kamaneva's shots. I can barely hold myself upright, because when I do, the world starts spinning and I begin losing my balance. I'm guessing that has something to do with the shock of a bullet entering my body. To say nothing of rapid blood loss.

This is not my best day. Or night.

"Alpha One!" I shout.

Our militiamen are actually pushing back against the Omega troops, forcing them towards the center of the field, cutting a hole in their lines. It's turned into an all out bloodbath. Soldiers are fighting hand to hand, tackling each other, jamming knives into each other's throats. I turn away from the gut-wrenching scene and find Chris in the thick of the battlefield. There's no way he can see me.

I make a desperate attempt to find cover, lunging behind an overturned vehicle. There's not much left of it besides a charred frame and some twisted metal, but it'll do. Kamaneva is still behind me, and I'm not in the mood to come face to face with one of her guns again. The third time is *so* not the charm.

I crawl on my hands and knees, bullets hitting the metal on the car, zipping right over my head. I scramble to the other side of the car and claw my way into the tall grass, blinking back tears of pain. My body feels like it's on fire, which can't be a good sign. I stumble upon a dead Omega soldier. His handgun is lying next to him. I pick it up and manage to climb to my feet, staggering far enough into the field to take cover behind a tree, pressing my back against the trunk. I spot Kamaneva. She's no more than thirty feet away, attempting to get to me without putting herself in the direct line of the fire from the battleground.

She glares and fires in my direction. I shift my position and make sure the tree shields my entire body. I'm safe for now, but not forever. I look at the gun in my hand, wondering if there's any ammo left. The battle is raging around me. An Omega trooper appears out of the grass and spots me. I react without thinking, snapping a round to his chest.

Yeah. There's ammo in it.

That's the second guy I've shot at close range today. I swallow the nausea and turn my attention to Kamaneva. What I really *need* to do is kill her, just like every other Omega soldier. I lift the gun, sighting her. It's not hard. She's exposing herself in order to reach me, and that will be the death of her.

But my hands are shaking and I'm having a hard time keeping the sights in the middle of her chest. I adjust the weapon, angry. I'm clutching my side with one hand, blood pouring between my fingers. The gun wavers in my other.

Just do it, I think. *This woman is* ***evil***. *She doesn't deserve mercy.*

Right?

A split second of hesitation is just about the worst thing you can do in the middle of a fight. Kamaneva ducks out of sight, disappearing into the tall grass. I lose her and keep a tight grip on my handgun, unable to stand by myself. All I've got left is the gun in my hand – and the ammo that's left inside it. Once I run out, I'm dead.

Kamaneva crawls out of the grass, slathered in mud and grime. She's filthy, and there's an expression on her face that can only be described as possessed. "Dead," she hisses.

I'm not sure whom she's referring to.

Herself, her daughter, or me.

Probably all three.

"You're about to be," I mutter.

She jerks backwards and hits the ground, her hand to her chest. I blink, memories resurfacing of Kamaneva getting shot by Max the last time she tried to kill me. And now red blood is blossoming in the center of her chest, getting bigger by the second. She gasps and stares at me in horror, coughing. Blood trickles out of the corner of her mouth.

She begins to say something – maybe it's something important, maybe not – but before she can get it out my attention is drawn to the right. A tall man walks out of the bushes. A militiaman dressed in dark brown camouflage, a broad rimmed hat pulled down over his forehead. His face is covered with a standard face scarf. He looks down at Kamaneva, kicking her weapon aside with his foot. He says nothing.

"Thank you," I say.

He turns to me and nods, and that's when I notice the white star etched into the sleeve of his jacket. It's a pretty crude depiction, but the shape is distinct. I force myself to my feet. "You're a *Mountain Ranger*," I realize.

"Yes, ma'am." His voice has a southern twang. "And you're a *Freedom Fighter*."

I say, "How are you here?"

He doesn't answer immediately. He drops to one knee.

"We got a tip," he replies. "And the boss said to come running."

I turn back to look at the hills. The yelling and gunfire has kicked up a notch and my anonymous *Mountain Ranger* friend disappears into the battle, leaving me alone with a dying Kamaneva. She's sputtering for air, turning to the side, trying to spit out the blood pooling in her mouth.

Harry has vanished.

I kneel next to her, too wired and wounded to find a boatload of sympathy for a woman who murdered hundreds – possibly thousands – of innocent men, women and children. And yet I still whisper," I'm sorry." She looks at me with wide, frightened eyes. An expression of disbelief crosses her face before she stares into the distance, her eyes going glassy.

Kamaneva is dead.

"Cassie!" Chris bursts out of the grass, grabbing my arm. He looks at Kamaneva. He looks at me.

"You've been shot." His expression tightens and he wraps an arm under my shoulders, dragging me away from the field.

"Where are we going?" I ask, clinging to him. My energy level is draining. "Chris!"

"We're losing, Cassie," he replies, moving behind the same

vehicle I just took cover under a few minutes ago. "You need to get inside the warehouse and stay safe."

He pulls back my jacket and lifts up my shirt, looking at my gunshot wound. His face betrays no emotion, but I can tell by the way he's clutching the material that whatever he's thinking doesn't have anything to do with positivity.

"I'm going to die, aren't I?" I state. "There's nothing you can do."

"No." He takes my face between his hands. "You are *not* going to die."

Another *Mountain Ranger* appears from the grass, distinguishable by his broad rim hat and white star on the sleeve of his jacket.

"Chris..." I mutter. "Are you seeing what I'm seeing?"

He doesn't let go of me, but he flicks his gaze towards the battlefield. A human wave of *Mountain Rangers* are pouring over the side of the hill, opening fire on Omega. Smoke is blanketing the entire field. Mortar rounds explode, sending bits of rock, glass and twisted metal into the sky. The constant roar of automatic gunfire permeates the air. The strong smell of gunpowder and burning vegetation is heavy.

"Who gave them the tip?" I wonder, awed.

Chris doesn't answer. Does it matter? Backup has arrived.

"Just stay with me," Chris commands. There's a hint of desperation in his voice. I lean forward and kiss him, tasting sweat and smoke against his mouth. He holds me with a death grip, breaking the kiss only when it's absolutely necessary. Both of us are breathing hard.

"Oh, that's a lovely sight. I'm going to gag now."

I snap my head around at the sound of a familiar voice. Chris's brother, Jeff, is standing behind us, decked out in full combat garb, his chest heaving with every breath. "Really, that was touching," he gasps. "But you might want to look *around.* The *Mountain Rangers* are here now."

"You're supposed to be guarding the camp," Chris growls. "How did you even...?" And then he drops it. There's a lot to explain, and sitting in the middle of the battlefield behind a broken car with a girl that's just been shot isn't the best place to have a heart-to-heart chat.

"Go," I urge, fighting to take a deep breath. "You need to be a leader right now. You can't do that if you're sitting here with me."

"Cassie, I won't leave you."

"You're not. Jeff is here." I touch the side of his face with my hand. "I love you."

Jeff kneels down next to me, nodding at his brother.

Chris squares his jaw and kisses me one more time.

"Keep her safe," he tells Jeff. It's not a request. He stands up and ducks into the tall grass, making his way back towards the battle zone. It's almost impossible to hear anything over the piercing noise of the fighting, but I make an attempt to figure out the situation anyway.

"How did you get here?" I ask Jeff.

"*Mountain Rangers* came into camp about an hour after you left." He shrugs. "They wanted to help us fight after all. So I brought them."

I purse my lips.

"Thank you," I say. "You got here in just in time."

Jeff takes a look at my wound and makes an effort to stop the bleeding, packing it with combat gauze, wrapping a tight bandage around my waist. He hands me a bottle of water and a couple of pills from a medical kit. I take a long drink and choke the pills down, gagging a few times in the process. Feeling faint, I put my head between my legs to try and stabilize the rush of blood from my brain. Jeff loosens my gear in an attempt to give me room to breathe. My body is going into shock and I need to keep it under control, otherwise I'll end up dead.

A few minutes – or maybe it's a few hours – later, Sophia returns, bruised and bloody. But she's still walking, which is a fairly positive sign. "We're pulling out," she pants. "Now." And then she sees my bloody shirt. "Oh, my God. Cassidy, what happened?"

"Kamaneva," I reply, trembling with the effort of staying conscious.

"She's *here*?"

"Was."

"Are you serious?" She helps Jeff haul me to my feet, and I lean heavily against him for support. My limbs are getting stiff. "I can't believe it."

"I can." I start coughing. "Jeff, be careful. Watch for mortar rounds."

We pull back into the side of the hill, putting distance between ourselves and the depot. Omega is coming towards us like a dark tide, killing everything in its path. Even with the extra *Mountain Rangers* filling the field, we're still being forced backwards.

Chris finds us in the midst of the chaos, grabbing me around the waist and holding me to his chest. He pushes me halfway behind his back, protecting me with his body as we retreat. And as we do, my eyes fall on the wide expanse of the battlefield. The white smoke has turned black, shrouding the scene. The open space is crawling with Omega troopers. And then the line stops, and our side is suddenly pushing back against Omega. It's a vicious game of tug-of-war. One side surges against the other. More people drop. Another surge. Another round of gunfire. More dying.

"Look!" Jeff exclaims, pointing.

Mountain Rangers are coming from behind the Omega troopers, pushing their way across the field, closing them in on two sides. What's left of our forces is joining with them, initiating Chris's backup plan. *Rangers* and *Freedom Fighters* form a ring around Omega's men, dropping to the ground, firing from hidden vantage points. Omega is completely surrounded, and what's more, they're being fired on from every direction. As they move forward, our forces move backwards, and the rest of the *Freedom Fighters* follow. Omega troops are trapped inside a giant circle of fire – and they panic.

The Omega soldiers scatter, confused. Running for their lives. There's no mistaking the terror in their voices as they scream frantic orders to their men, trying to stay alive as the fire rains down on them from all directions. And here I am on the sidelines, contributing to the firefight, taking out one trooper at a time with my commandeered pistol despite my gunshot wound. Alexander Ramos staggers through the madness, making his way towards us. He stumbles and falls. Chris moves to help him, but he's beaten to it by a *Mountain Ranger*. This one has an eagle feather in his hat – the only deviation from the standard broad rim hat I've been seeing on the *Rangers* all night. He puts his arm under Alexander's shoulders and drags him through the firefight to the sidelines, not far away from my position.

The Omega troopers are scattered and on the run. Our forces are left with an opening to retreat, so we move out. Our men move back into the side of the hill, firing on the enemy as we pull away.

Our forces retreat to the other side of the mountain as the *Rangers* take care of business down below in the field, drawing what's left of Omega's forces away from our depleted ranks. Our trucks are close. If we can reach them, we can get the wounded back to camp before it's too late. We've already lost so many soldiers, though…

"Cassie, stay with me," Chris says, shaking my shoulders. "Come on."

I'm zoning out. I feel the cool metal of the pickup truck under my fingers and make a monumental effort to focus my vision. Our troops are piling onto the pickup beds as fast as they can, hauling the wounded along with them. I guess I'm one of them. Chris lifts me into his arms and lays me across the seat in the cab, gunning the engine. I close my eyes, licking the blood off my lips.

God, what's happened to me?

A few seconds pass. Orders are exchanged. Chris floors it. We take off into the night, leaving the battlefield. But it's not over yet. Omega patrols are out in full force, sweeping the highways and combing through the underbrush. And where do we go? If Harry betrayed us to Omega, doesn't that mean he told them where our camp was? Are the Youngs and the rest of the camp being raided by Omega troopers right now? How can we go back?

I have so many questions.

"All right, up we go..." Chris pulls me into a sitting position, pressing his hand against my side. Something breaks in his voice. "Don't let go, Cassie."

Jeff is standing on the running board outside the door. He helps pull me out of the cab.

"What are we doing?" I ask, dizzy.

"We have to hoof it," Chris replies. "The roads are blocked. Too many patrols."

"It's too far," I say.

"We can do it."

Well, *they* can. I'll just curl up in a ball and die right here, thank you very much. Yet something in the back of my mind says: *Don't let go. Don't give up.*

I force myself to keep my eyes open as Chris supports me with his body. I feel like I'm inside out. I'm hot, lightheaded. Everything is too loud and too fast.

What I would give to pick up the phone and call 911.

"Alpha One?" someone calls for Chris.

A patrol is moving towards us from across the road. The gunfire from the battlefield is still audible from the other side of the hill. Our troops fall into formation to stop the patrol. My heart sinks. There's no escape, is there?

"Hey, are you Alpha One?"

Chris turns. A platoon of *Rangers* are moving towards us from across the road. The *Mountain Ranger* with the feather in his cap approaches Chris at the front of the group, his rifle in his hands. His face is obscured behind a scarf, and the only thing distinguishable about his appearance is his eyes.

"Eagle One?" Chris asks.

"At your service."

Eagle One.

The codename for the leader of the Mountain Rangers?

It has to be. Looks like Chris is going to get his pow-wow after all. I sag against him, spent. I can't go any farther.

I just *can't.*

"Cassidy?" Eagle One takes a step towards us. Chris tenses, ready to defend me. An explosion of automatic gunfire deafens the world around us. The moon is shining brightly against the dark sky, illuminating the foothills, giving the landscape an alien appearance.

"*Cassidy Hart,*" Eagle One says, the voice familiar through the haze of pain. He's pulling off his scarf, moving towards me. Chris pushes me behind him, taking a defensive stance. Eagle

One drops his rifle to the ground and opens his arms up, the scarf rolled up in his hands.

A wave of shock ripples through me. My eyes focus long enough to recognize his face. It's *him*. Familiar brown eyes, laugh lines around the mouth, a military haircut under the broad rim hat. It can't be. I have to be hallucinating.

I stare, openmouthed, only able to form a single word:

"Dad?"

I reach out to him just as the world around me starts to spin.

Everything goes black.

Epilogue

War sucks. Sure, it's kind of necessary right now, but that doesn't mean I have to like it. Last year, the only thing I would have known about warfare is what I'd seen in the movies or watched on the news. It was something imaginary. Something that didn't really exist because I'd never personally experienced it.

The EMP changed everything.

How did I jump from being a struggling high school graduate to a guerilla warfighter in a turf war against an invading army? How did I end up falling in love with Chris? How did I end up surviving the EMP? How did I survive the first wave of Omega's invasion forces when millions of other people died?

How? Why?

I feel like my life is nothing but a series of question marks. There's so much we *don't* know about Omega, but does it matter? They're bad, and we're good. The *Freedom Fighters* are doing the job that nobody else can or will do. We're fighting back against tyranny. We're taking a stand. This is our home. Nobody can take it away from us without a fight.

When I first met Chris last year, I told him that if he tried to hurt me, I'd shoot him right between the eyes. But I didn't mean it. I didn't know what I was doing. I was a scared teenager trying to survive a terrifying attack on Los Angeles. I'd never been in a fight in my life. I never would have been able to defend myself.

Now I can.

So I guess the question is, what's next? We can't fight Omega forever...can we? I mean, how long can guerilla forces hide out in the foothills and attack Omega? Would we be better off just giving up and assimilating into Omega's new society? Or should we keep fighting...even if the odds are against us?

I know what Chris's answer would be. The same as mine.

We can't give up. We have something worth fighting *for.* Our families, our homes, our freedom. Normalcy. Those things are precious. Priceless. I never realized how great my life was until everything got taken away. I guess that'll teach me to take things for granted. Living as a nomad in the wilderness puts things in perspective real fast.

So we'll keep fighting anyway. Not because it's fun. Not because it's easy. Because it's the right thing to do. And really, that's what it all comes down to, isn't it? Doing the right thing.

I won't give up hope, because that's all we have left. Hope keeps us going. Believing in something bigger than ourselves. To give up would be suicidal, and personally, I'm not crazy about the idea of dying. Not yet. I've still got some fight left in me. We all do.

Omega's about to find out the hard way.

To Be Continued in

State of Rebellion

Book 3 of the Collapse Series

More Titles from Summer Lane:

The Collapse Series

State of Emergency

State of Chaos

State of Rebellion

State of Pursuit

State of Alliance

State of Vengeance

State of Destruction

State of Fear

State of Allegiance

State of Hope

The Zero Trilogy

Day Zero

Day One

End of Day

The Bravo Saga

Bravo: Apocalypse Mission

Bravo: Blood Road

Graphic Companions

Collapse: The Illustrated Guide

And the standalone hit:

Unbreakable SEAL

About the Author

Summer Lane is the #1 bestselling author of the *Collapse Series, Zero Trilogy, Bravo Saga, Collapse: The Illustrated Guide* and the adventure thriller, *Unbreakable SEAL.*

Summer owns WB Publishing. She is an accomplished journalist and creative writing teacher. She also owns an online magazine, Writing Belle, where she has interviewed and worked with countless authors from around the globe.

Summer lives in the Central Valley of California with her husband, where she enjoys reading, collecting tea, visiting the beach and the mountains, and counting down the days until she has her very own puppy (if you've read *Bravo: Apocalypse Mission,* you'll understand).

Connect with Summer online at:

Summerlaneauthor.com

WritingBelle.com

Twitter: @SummerEllenLane

Facebook: @SummerLaneAuthor

Email Summer with thoughts or comments at:

summerlane101@gmail.com

Acknowledgements

State of Chaos.

If I could describe the experience of writing a book in any three words possible, *State of Chaos* would be it. Creating a story and publishing it is one of the most challenging projects that you can ever undertake. *State of Chaos* was penned in May and April of 2013, and it was not done without the help and support of many wonderful people. I originally began work on the story in February 2013, and decided to hold off on finishing it until I completed some valuable research to add a whole new level of authenticity to Cassidy Hart's story.

During those months, my dad was instrumental in helping fine-tune the structural organization of the *Freedom Fighters.* Chris Young is a brilliant leader because my dad is.

Thanks for everything!

My mother, brother and grandparents were wonderfully supportive during the creation of *State of Chaos,* as well. For the research aspects of the novel, I had a huge helping hand from Scott Brandt and Joseph Krahn. Their invitation to the *Project Appleseed* program funded by the RWVA gave me the hands-on experience I needed to give Cassidy Hart a fighting advantage. It's safe to say that *both* Cassidy and I learned a lot.

I am truly grateful to God for the success of the *Collapse Series,* and as Cassidy Hart's adventures continue, I can only buckle down and get ready for the rest of the ride!

Psalm 118:24